# imaginary *friends*

written by
joshua crocker

IMAGINARY FRIENDS



ISBN: 979-8-9879131-3-0 (paperback)

Library of Congress Control Number: 2026911103

Cover design by Joshua Crocker.

Page design by Joshua Crocker.

Paperback print. B&W edition 2026.

Written by Joshua Crocker.
Norman, OK
paragoncoalition.com

## My Other Books

One Day I'll Know

Snippets of Ink

Songs About Self-Defense

November Storm

Oh No, Another Homemade Christmas Present

*dedicated to*

*jake, james, payton, and tagen*

# Table of Contents

## Content Advisory

This story explores certain topics and themes some may be sensitive to. This includes depression, religion + faith, sexuality, substance use, fighting + violence, abuse, and explicit language. Please read with care.

"I guess I'm scared that I'm imaginary. That I reinvent myself every day, so other people don't have to. That who I am is secondary to what I want everyone else to see. And I'm scared that I'm crazy, but God help me, I'm twice as scared I'm sane. 'Cause then what excuse do I have for treating people like problems that need to be solved or explained?"

– Matt Johnston,
*The Narcissist Cookbook*

# November Storm

# Waiting on a Storm

I hate the feeling of waiting on a storm.
The anxiety builds in my stomach
for things I have little control over.
As I went to bed Halloween night,
I had the same feeling in my mind.
There's nothing like a November storm.

I feel nauseous, to be fair, I haven't been eating well.
Life has been more chaotic as of late,
there are tornadoes in the fall, voting lines have begun,
and I've been staying up way too late.
You can't rhyme 'late' with 'late'.
I'm worried over more things than I can count.
Sorry Jesus, but that whole 'Do-Not-Be-Anxious' thing
hasn't been working out for me.

The skies are uniquely gray, it's beautiful really.
The wind picks up the falling leaves
and scatters them around town.
I know this week will be a hectic one,
and the one after that will likely also be.
By the time Thanksgiving Day gets here
I don't even know what I'll be saying thanks for.

Some things just don't make sense to me.
People like me are praying for the country,
but we've been casting our ballots differently.
Wasn't it just last night we were all
hiding in our closets from a storm?
But then the very next day you go out
and cheer for something way worse.

A moment ago the sun peaked out from the clouds.
It hid away again soon after.
If that isn't a metaphor for something, what is.
I'm even fearful of the things that make me happy.
Like that nervous feeling you get around a pretty girl.
I've been trying to impress this woman
who probably just sees me as a friend.
I want to make her laugh, but I keep stuttering instead.
When I smiled the other day, did anyone notice?
Most of all, did she notice?
Or like the sun, do I hide away too soon?

I'm sitting in the dark, waiting on a storm.
Trying to write some words that reflect how I feel.
Why should I worry over the things I can't control?
I don't pray as much as I should.
Or maybe my prayers are just misunderstood.
I've walked more miles to nowhere than I'm aware of.
The rain has begun to fall from above,
and I feel anxious of what's to come.
I keep walking down the street regardless,
preparing my thoughts for the month ahead.
Thoughts of hope and dread.
There's nothing like a November storm.

# Friendships on Hold

Where did you go?
Let me just say, it's true.
You don't realize what you got, till you don't.
One, two, three, probably more.
While you're drowning in homework and job
applications, I'm drowning my feelings in music.
We've got so much to talk about,
but you don't have the time to be my therapist.
And I'd rather complain than solve the issue.
I look for you when I go for walks,
I'm still waiting for a text back,
we never did find a time to grab drinks.
One, two, three, probably more.
Is it too cliché to say I miss you?
What's worse, I don't know if I do.
Were we ever all that close?
Did I ever actually think about you
outside of the context of myself?
I don't know if I ever really did.
After a couple days of not seeing you, I moved on.
Did it even take you that long?
One, two, three, probably more, friendships on hold.

# Delirious

After 9:30 I start to get a little delirious.
Maybe I'll zone out or doze off a bit.
I'm not built for college late nights.
Or maybe I'm just not built for real life.
The pressure is too much for me.

When I reread this in the morning it will be nonsense.
I haven't been thinking right all day,
and all the nervousness has broken me.
When I try to remember what I said or who I am,
all I know is the memories won't reflect the same.

I think you've gotten a little delirious too.
While I sit here quietly losing my mind,
you outwardly are losing all sense of sanity.
I can sit back and watch, I laugh, but inside I'm not.
Because my eyes can only see what my head says it can.

The clock ticks closer to 10:00, and I'm a little delirious.
Nothing makes sense anymore, did it ever really?
My imagination hates me more than anyone else does.
I should just accept I'm my own worst enemy.
The pressure is just too much for me.

# I Want To Believe

I want to believe that God's people are good.
Jesus, I want to believe that you loved everyone,
but my brothers and sisters don't seem to think so.
I want to go to church and sing songs of grace,
not question if I belong in these worship halls.
I don't need all the facts, that ain't my style,
I just need something to believe in,
and I need y'all to believe in me.

I want to believe that all prayers are heard.
Jesus, I want to believe that you live still,
but the words my friends read are increasingly shallow.
I want to go to church and learn about spirituality,
not pretend to be the same as I was at seventeen.
I don't understand why we can't have real conversations,
but instead must justify everything through old scrolls,
none of us willing to think any differently.

I want to believe. I want to believe in the stories.
I want to believe in God's love.
I want to believe all people can have a voice.
I want to believe. I want to believe this can be my home.

# All It Takes

All it takes is a smile and compliment
and I know I'm screwed.
It's been a week now and I'm still not sure what to do.
I won't say I'm crushing,
but that would explain the blushing.
I keep doing this to myself, so here we go again.
You called me smart,
but I'm dumb when it comes to the heart.
I keep glancing your way; you're just nice to look at.
There's no way this ends well,
but there's only one way to tell.
I'm trying to find the right words to say, but hey,
maybe a smile and conversation with you is all it takes.

There's so much to say
that I don't know where to begin

I could write for hours *i tend to*
but I'll stare at a blank screen instead

It feels like
I'm walking through the fog,
and I'm not lost,

just confused

I'm questioning

my faith
the time of day
who I am
my own thoughts

a lot of things

Sleep has become a blessing
not a commodity

Restless at night Restless during the day

And the worst part is

I love it

this is what I've been writing about

I don't care about the meaning,

just the theatrics

things could be terrible, but at least they're alive

poets are fueled by stories
that they can twist and turn
until they've lost all feeling

they're just words
and words are just memories

but when they ask me where I've been

I can tell them I've been walking in the fog

I just fear

that the fog will swallow me up

before I reach
the other side

but for now, I'm going to keep pace,
rummaging for a lighter

and if I can find a flame to follow
then the fog is no more than a brush with the sky

*I just sat there, in disbelief. I mean, this was always a possibility, but I still wasn't prepared. I went to bed without saying word. At that point I had accepted it was over. When I woke up, the world just felt, well, sad. I went for a walk to try and comprehend it all, but I just kept coming back to the same conclusion. I was wrong. I had believed something that I wanted to believe, but I had ignored reality. As I took in my surroundings, everything looked different. It felt like I had finally realized the truth, and now, the world as I knew it just seemed different.*

# Sadness

Walking down University Boulevard
is a girl with a sadness in her eyes.
Her blank stare tells more than enough.
She's not angry or mad or even upset,
just sad, unsure of what comes next.

Her eyes express a brokenness deep inside.
Last night something in her heart had died.
She had been fighting for so long,
but still lost in the end.
Worse than any loss,
was the truth she now believed.
She had always said people were inherently good,
this truth she had held for so long was now gone.
Her faith in humanity had vanished in her sleep.

Her eyes give way to a thousand words.
A prayer of mourning for her sisters,
for words that would never be enough.
A poem of sorrow for herself,
for her existence had been denied.

There's a girl with a sadness in her eyes.
No tears, no words to say.
She knew she would never be the same.
Her heart wrote the eulogy for her younger self,
the girl who had still believed in goodness.
What comes next is still uncertain.
I hope she keeps fighting,
finds a way to heal the sadness in her eyes.

# Sitting in the Dark

I was lying in bed this morning, counting down the seconds until my phone told me to get up.

When the alarm finally went off, I begrudgingly got up and checked my notifications.

About ten minutes earlier my town was under a tornado warning, and I hadn't heard a thing.

Why are these times so strange?
Humans are acting more like robots
and the robots are more humanlike.
There are April showers in November
and I just keep sitting in the dark.

I got up and turned on the news, muting it while I prepared myself some breakfast.

I drove to a nearby coffee shop to work on this book, but as I opened my word doc, the power went out.

Now I'm here, surrounded by a handful of other people, writing alone in a dimly lit room.

Why are these times so strange?
Humans are acting more like robots
and the robots are more humanlike.
There are April showers in November
and I just keep sitting in the dark.

# Sun

The storm is over now.
I can still see the puddles,
at least the twisters have left.
Until next year anyway.

The sun is out now.
What a beautiful morning,
I've never felt so miserable.
Is this some cruel joke?

The sky is quiet now.
I rather go back to the howling winds
than listen to this eerie silence.
Anxiety is better than defeat.

The storm is over now.
The rain and wind may be done,
but the worst is yet to come.
Watch the sun rise over these dark times.

# Sad Stuff

So, I was talking with my cousin.
Told her I was writing a book.
She asked me about what. I said sad stuff.
And she was like, why sad stuff?
And I was like, why not?
It's funny how much I enjoy the misery.
She was like, you're weird.
And I was like, well thank you.

I've been known for a few things,
one being I can be a little dramatic.
I act all traumatic, I'm playing it up.
I'm not lying, per say, just embellishing.

So, I was talking with my cousin.
She asked if I'm okay. I said I've never been better.
I was like, you want to hear something sad?
And she was like, why would I?

Let's also get one thing clear,
most of the stories aren't even that sad.
Half of these pages are just ramblings
about my family, crushes, and a pet ladybug.
But who cares about that?
I just care about the sad stuff.

So, I was talking with my cousin.
I said writing about sad stuff makes the stuff seem less sad.
She was like, and how is that?
And I was like, I always seem to tie it back to hope.
And she was like, well I would hope you do.
I've been known for a few things,
one being my unrelenting optimism.
She was like, I still love you, but you're kinda weird.
And I was like, well I wouldn't want it any other way.

# Isolationism

I'm an introverted kind of person.
I like to have time to myself.
I still feel lonely from time to time though.
It's not just that I miss my friends,
but more that I feel like I'm taking on life alone.
There will be someone who reads this
who feels the same away.
Here's what I want you to know:
You're not in this alone.
I've seen the sadness in people's eyes.
I hear the fear in your voices.
I've seen tornado wreckage before,
I've watched the streets begin to flood,
but the worst feeling when a storm is near
is knowing I'm alone with nowhere to go.
When the storm of our life is on the way,
don't let yourself feel isolated.
My theory is that the people that hate you
want you to feel alone, they want you scared.
In a system of isolationism
you're more likely to fall in line.
Don't give in. Don't hide.
And maybe I'm not the one to give this advice.
I've spent the entire year doing just this.
I was angry at people I shouldn't have been.
But y'know what, it didn't help.
I've realized I'm happier when I let people love me.
A thing that seems obvious to me now.
So, when a storm is near, don't isolate yourself.
You weren't made to take on life alone.
Let yourself be happy still. Let yourself be loved.
It won't make the storm go away,
but it'll make the wind feel more like a breeze.

# Distracted

Damnit, I've been a bit distracted lately.
I've been bringing my dreams with me when I wake,
tired from all the hem and hawing as I'm toss and turning.
Can't even finish a simple task without getting a little
sidetracked. I guess I'm not complaining though.

I told myself in the moment I wouldn't overthink this,
but I've been playing another round of
my favorite game, Is She Being Friendly or Flirting?
The answer is always there's no way to tell.
That won't stop me from replaying the footage on loop.
The way you smiled and rubbed my shoulder
and the stupid ways I find to make a fool of myself.

It's all the time, I'm habitual overanalyzer,
too quick to write love stories in my mind,
too slow to say the words I already designed.

I write some things down.
I claim these feelings will make for a great book.
I don't know if that's true.
These poems are less art, more me decompressing.

Why do you have to be so distracting?
I guess I have always been one to get
distracted by something pretty.

# Social Hangover

Did you sleep well last night?
Well, I could have slept worse.
Feeling hungover without ever taking a drink.
Drinking away what should have been a great time.
I've always thought I didn't have the social battery
to be around people for a long time,
but maybe I don't have the mental capacity
to eat breakfast alone the next morning.
My mind races, completely overthinking.
Thinking through every damn thing.
Every time I touch the memories
they turn a little more blue.
But none of that's even true.
As soon as I roll out of bed I let the TV think for me.
Open a jar of peanut butter to help heal me.
Did you have fun last night?
Funny enough, I don't even know.
Anytime I let my heart start beating,
the next day it'll be head that's beating.

# Not Enough

I mumbled my words when I said you were cute.
It seems the awkward glances only go one way.
This could be something more, but I've already
decided if I ask you out, you'll just say no.

If I were just a little funnier, you would laugh more,
and if I was just a little hotter, you would be blushing.
If I was just a little better, then maybe. But I'm not.

I'm not enough for you.
I'm not strong enough, I'm not tall enough.
There's nothing that makes me special.
I'm not clever enough, I'm not charming enough.
At least I'm not stupid enough to think you
think about me the same way I think about you.

Sitting at the girl's table listening to them talk smack.
'No offense,' you say. Don't patronize me.
I'm glad you remembered I was here,
cause it seems I have a tendency to be invisible
until I decide to make a fool of myself.

*Go back to being a happily alone doll in denial.*
*This constant 'will she, won't I' makes you sound senile.*

I'm better at being a brother than a boyfriend,
that's where my experience is at.
I make a great side character in any friend group,
but I shouldn't fool myself into thinking
I'll ever be the star. Cause I'm not.

If I were just a little funnier, you would laugh more,
and if I was just a little hotter, you would be blushing.
If I was just a little better, then maybe. But I'm not.

I'm not enough for you.
I'm not strong enough, I'm not tall enough.
There's nothing that makes me special.
I'm not clever enough, I'm not charming enough.
At least I'm not stupid enough to think you
think about me the same way I think about you.

Now it's my turn to say, 'no offense.'
What makes a girl like you so worth this beatdown?
Whenever I try to imagine us together,
I can only ever see my worst qualities.
In frustration, I yell back at the voices in my head,
but deep down I know I'm telling myself
exactly what I want to hear.

*You're not enough. You'll never be enough.*
*You're just a loser with loser feelings too.*
*You're not enough. You'll never be enough.*
*Enough of a friend. Enough of a man.*
*Enough of a human being.*
*You're just a rough draft of someone else.*
*And that'll never be enough.*

It doesn't matter what you say.
I've already told myself I'm not enough.

# The Need to Apologize

Dear Jenna, I feel the need to apologize.
For what, I don't know why.
I know you're not mad at me.
In fact, you've been nothing but kind.
But Jenna, I've been too hard on myself lately.
It's cliché, yet I feel tugged in every direction.
I'm obsessed with the people and things
that don't seem to be worth my time.
Jenna, I'm sorry. I don't want to let you down.
It seems the more I write, the more I forget.
I'm too smart to just let myself fall apart.
But I'm too young to do anything else.

Dear Joshua, do you know I love you?
It seems you forget that too often.
When I see you, I just feel compassion.
I know how tiring these days have been for you.
But Joshua, you can't keep hating yourself.
You say you don't, but I hear the way you talk.
Let yourself be happy with the people and things
that surround you, just stop obsessing over time.
Joshua, it'll be okay. You're not going to let me down.
The more we walk together, the more we understand.
Don't let me or anyone else take over your life.
We're too young to know everything.

Dear Jenna, I feel I've been lying to you.
Maybe worse, I abandoned you.
I've been lying to everyone, most of all myself.
I rather fantasize about my little stories.
Jenna, it seems I've lost the plot.

Dear Joshua, I see through all the nonsense.
You know I'm not going anywhere.
I think the worst lie you've told yourself
is that you have to choose what happens next.
Joshua, life is more complex than one story.

Dear Jenna, can I be vulnerable with you?
I don't know how to keep up with all this.
I never thought real life would be so complicated.
I've been writing in overtime to process it all.
Jenna, I've been struggling lately.

Dear Joshua, I'll always be there for you.
Who said you had to keep up with all this?
Real life isn't a battle to win, it's a journey.
Your words are better said than kept away.
Joshua, it's okay to struggle. That's just a part of life.

# Busy Body

Deadlines will be the death of me.
Meetings, videos to edit, pages to revise.
Please don't forget to DM me in the morning.
Once you're done eating breakfast
it'll be time for lunch.
Didn't have time to shave again,
forgot to click save and send.
Creative projects are fun till they're not.
I love being productive, but I hate being busy.

# An Outlandish Request

I just wanted to live without fear.
Was I too demanding?
Was it unfair of me to expect more from you all?
I would take a compromise.
I would even admit I was wrong at times,
but this means more than petty disagreements.
Is this the best we can do?
I just wanted to protect my family and friends.
In the future, how will I explain this to my kids?
Is this lying, racism, and stupidity
really represent who we are?
I thought we were smarter than that?
Maybe I was the one who was ignorant all along.
Give me anyone, give me anything,
just don't give me a hateful, spiteful, evil dirtbag.
Is that too much to ask?

# These Are Just Thoughts

I don't understand the point anymore.
I've poured my heart out.
I was patient, I said sorry, I said thanks.
But these are just thoughts.
If you were listening, I couldn't tell.
Maybe all you did was nod your head
and mutter a few words under your breath.
I tried to not be entitled,
but at best this is just self-meditation.
I've told you things that maybe
are better shared with a therapist.
Ask and it shall be given, seek and you shall find,
all I've been doing is working the equation in my mind.
When I'm done speaking with you
all I hear is echoing silence.
Maybe I'm just angry,
but when the bad guys have won,
and I'm still facing the same anxieties I always have,
I start to wonder what the point ever was.
Did I ask for too much?
I wanted to be a better person,
make the world a happy place.
I wanted to be loved,
not afraid of life anymore.
But those were just thoughts.

# Angry Acquaintance Phase

At best we exchange awkward small talk,
with nothing much to chat about.
We used to go on and on forever.
What happened to change that?

You used to be someone I could trust in,
you were my family, my friends,
but that has come to an end.
I no longer believe in you.
We loved each other, at least we pretended to.
But just because I knew you when I was a kid
doesn't mean I have to follow after you.
I have enough evidence to know
you don't really care about me.
You were my family, my friends,
now we're just acquaintances passing by.

The words don't add up.
You contradict yourself in every conversation.
We may smile and greet each other to keep peace,
but what was the last real thing we said to one another?
It's not my fault I've matured
while you've stayed the same.

You used to be someone I could trust in,
you were my family, my friends,
but that has come to an end.
I no longer believe in you.
I'm not trying to say anyone is at fault here,
I think you and I are just fundamentally different people.
So, can we just let this go?
Stop believing a lie, pretending we still get along.
You were my family, my friends,
now we're just acquaintances passing by.

# God Above

Have you turned away from this wicked place yet?
Forsaken us like we've forsaken you.
You gave us dominion over the seas and sky,
why is it everything we touch seems to die?
Do you stay away because your creation
has become too powerful and destructive?

God above,
do certain people deserve to live on the street?
My love,
can more bombs really lead to peace?
God above,
are our bodies made to be a prison cell?
My love,
does our endless pain really serve us well?

God, what would you say about us?
If you hadn't given your word,
would you send another flood?
How long is it before we cause
our own extinction event?
It only took two generations before
we learned to kill each other;
now we've learned to kill everything.

God above,
do certain people deserve to die alone?
My love,
what is kindness if it is not shown?
God above,
are our hearts meant to betray fate?
My love,
does our endless shouting reach heaven's gate?

I once believed no matter their faith
you made humans in good faith.
We were supposed to be a loving race,
but I think if there was proof without
a shadow of doubt that you were real,
our first reaction would be to build a weapon
so powerful that we could kill God himself.

I don't understand why,
why you haven't left us for good.
Is it just a sunk cost fallacy?
What promise do you still see in us?
Please tell me, because I don't see it.
It seems to me hate is stronger than love.
God above,
are we really the best life has to show?

# Run Away

Some days I dream of the places I'll run away to
on the day I leave you all behind.
I'll live in a place where it's freezing cold in November
and I won't have to worry about thunderclouds.
The bitter autumn wind as frigid as I am.
I won't even say goodbye.
Just pack up and skip town.
You won't even know why.
I won't talk much about my past.
Too proud to admit I miss my home.

Some days I don't think I'll be missed much
when I finally stop talking to you.
I could count on one hand the reasons to stay,
with the other hand in a guard as I back away.
I'll cut ties with all my friends,
caring about y'all was just too much.
The only number I'll keep is Izzy's,
text her when I miss my old life.
I'll tell mom to not worry when I send her a letter,
my new address on the envelope.
You can come and visit whenever you want.
Maybe I'll mail dad a copy of my next book,
my picture staring at you on the cover.
You can read it or not, whatever you want.

Some days I want to get as far away as I can,
a place where I'll be able to forget about it all.
I often pay more attention to the press
than what's actually in front of me.
I start to say things I never really meant.
I don't know if I'm frustrated or overwhelmed.
This is all too little; this can't be all life has to offer.
There has to be a place out there better than this.

Some days I might wonder if I was too hasty
back on the day I decided to leave it all behind.
If I ever return home no one will recognize me.
It'll have been ten, twenty years,
and I'll hardly look the same.
As I walk the same streets I did at nineteen,
I won't even know what to feel.
Nostalgia, hate, or regret. I don't want to know.
This place was never the same without me.

Some days it feels I'm counting down the days
until I finally get up and run away.
Pack my laptop, clothes, and everyday necessities.
I'll send my black belt, books, and Peter Pan doll
in a box to my new residence.
Life was just too much and too little here.
I care too much about these streets.
I think too much about where the ends meet.
I'd rather just run away from it all,
not have to think about it anymore.
I seem too little to roll with the punches.
I feel too little inside when I pray next to you.
I'd rather just run away from you all,
not have to think about you anymore.

Some days I just want to run away,
you know in that scared way I always get
whenever faced with the realities of life.
I'm so afraid of so many things,
and it seems so easy to just flee.
Deep down, I know I'll never do it.
Past my fears, I'm not ready to say goodbye.
Life can seem so hard some days,
but this is still my home.
And I'm not going anywhere.

# Vague

Sitting in the art gallery is a piece deemed abstract.
Is it cowardice or inspired that the artist
left their name anonymous?
A masterpiece of the reader's creation.
It comes across as pretentious and presumptuous,
an underlying fear of one's numbness.

I've left the poems and stories fairly vague.
You can't offend those you don't speak directly to.
I said this would be my most honest piece yet,
but there's nothing here.
The unnamed victims of my storytelling
are nothing more than creations of my imagination.

I said I wouldn't get political,
is that because I've realized I don't stand for anything?
I promised to not be crude,
is that because I fear people don't like me enough already?
I refuse to be personal,
is that because I can't handle the vulnerability?

Paint a self-portrait the way you want them to see it.
Leave out the blemishes that don't comply with life.
Rewrite and rewrite until the words are without meaning.
Hide your true feelings in the pages no one reads.
When I give this book to you as a gift
I don't want it to be the last one I give you.
But now it's just another knick-knack
collecting dust in the corner of your room.
The words entirely too vague, the meaning unclear,
an unfortunate representation of who I am to you.

# Lies, Eyes, and My Disguise

I say, "I'm not hungry. I ate before I arrived."
These are the words I repeat so many times.
What is true when all you see is fictionalized?

I say, "I hope you have a great rest of your week."
Tonight we both seemed rather quiet and meek.
I had more I wanted to say, like to ask if you're okay.

"Hey, I never realized how skinny you are," they say.
I don't know whether to say thanks or walk away.
There isn't a problem if I just ignore the signs.

They laugh, "Oh, it's you. I thought you were a girl."
Well, none of us are anything in this changing world.
What else did you expect me to say in return?

"You're so pretty," I say, but only inside my head.
I don't say it aloud, my eyes just follow you instead.
What is a lie if it's always by omission?

They say, "Are you hungry? You haven't eaten in a while."
These are the words repeated to me without a smile.
What am I so afraid of that I feel the need to hide?

# Jupiter and Saturn

Jupiter eyes Saturn
from across galaxy waves.
Her rings glow in the starlight,
luminating her face in the sky's night.
He hides behind his satellites,
afraid his mind isn't on right.
Gravity pulls them around,
friends of the mighty sun.
The two pass by on their paths,
Jupiter hums and Saturn laughs,
her beauty in the sky is unmatched.
He aches from his core around her,
full of nervous gas and shaky ground.
Jupiter eyes Saturn
from across galaxy waves.
She's brighter than a star in the night sky,
but he's just a rock floating right by.

# Afterthought

I have a list of people who mean a lot to me.
The people who I think about all the time.
Even when I'm bored or tired,
they're still on my mind.

How often do you think of me?
Call this fear irrational, people say the same about me,
but I fear I care more about you than you do me.
You only want to hang out when it's convenient for you.
I'm not demanding you to carve time
out of your busy schedule for me,
but it would be nice if you went a little
bit out of your way occasionally.
Or at least, say hi to me.
Why should I always have to be the one
to initiate a conversation?
Am I just an extra on the set of your life?
Because that's how it feels.
I get it, you have problems you're dealing with, so do I.
But on your priority list, I don't even make the top 25.
I think about you all the time,
do you know that?
Do you even give me a passing thought?
If so, it doesn't feel like it.

I tend to say I think too much,
but why don't you think of me at all?
You mean the world to me,
but to you, I'm just an afterthought.

# Illogical

I was only loosely paying attention in school,
now remind me what four plus three equals?
Is it an eight or a seven?

I was only loosely paying attention in church,
now remind me what the meaning of life is?
Can I create my own heaven?

I don't know.

It's illogical to think without breathing.
You'll pass out. I thought that was obvious.

My ideas and schemes are more insane by the day.
It's like refusing to get paid for all your hard work.
The thespian who can't tell reality from a work of fiction.
It's like listening to the same songs till they lose meaning.
The lesbian who tries to pick up girls at a Bible study.
It's like doing math and expecting the answer to change.

Is this insanity or a logical fallacy?
My heart has decided to ignore my brain
if it doesn't like what it has to say.

What's the point of baking a cake that you can't eat?
Okay, I lied. I don't even like cake.

I act like it's illogical to breathe without thinking.
No wonder I'm so tired all the time.
It's like thinking that a falling tree doesn't make a sound.

It's just illogical.

# Compliments

I have this weird conundrum where the more I care about
someone, the harder it is to show them.
I've said so many nice things about you in my head,
but can never seem to compliment you when I should.
Am I incapable of encouragement
if I'm not being paid for it?
Because it's starting to seem the only way I know
how to be personable is through martial arts.

Have I ever actually told my mom how much I look up to her?
Do I ever tell my dad I love him except when I'm leaving?
The only time I get close to people
is when I'm throwing them to the ground.
Do my brothers know how much I enjoy hanging out together?
Do my sisters realize I'd be there whenever they need me?
It's so much easier to be encouraging
after I get done kicking a person in the head.
I don't think I ever say thank you to my friends anymore.
I've never actually told a girl I find her pretty before.
It took me an entire hour to work up
the words to just say I like your jacket.

I have this weird conundrum where I forget
you can't read my thoughts about you.
I think so highly of so many people,
but I don't know if that always comes across clearly.
Am I incapable of complimenting people without a joke?
Because it's starting to seem the only way I know
how to be personable is through rambling poetry.

I have this tendency to think instead of speaking.
I think I like to overcomplicate being human.
I just hope I can learn to compliment people more.

*Hey, I'm glad you're here, you look nice today.*

# Ladybug

Love and loss seem to me to be intrinsically tied.
I've spent years trying to avoid having my heart broken.
I'm so scared of being sad, I tried to burn any feeling at all.
This is an ode to a ladybug, my Lady.

My relationship with the truth is contentious at best.
I've always said poets are the kings of lying.
Real life is far too much for me to handle,
I'd rather only ever tell a story,
because then I get to choose how it ends.

If I'm honest with you, let you how I'm feeling,
I run the risk of you leaving.
Instead, let's just stay in a state of casual familiarity,
where the way we feel isn't quite clear.
You can't be hurt if you never get close to anything.

I didn't know how to handle losing you so soon.
Took me years to treat it as anything more than a cruel joke.
I've forgotten more people than I remember.
It seems every year I lose touch with another friend.
I don't see the point in getting close
if they all leave eventually.

I've been trying to only ever live in the story I write,
all the while forgetting to live my life.
I'm done being afraid to leave my house,
afraid of losing the things that I care about.
If you do leave, I at least want you to know I loved you.
And if you stay, we can write this story together.

Growing older is learning to let go.
To a ladybug, my Lady, love to you.

# Cruce to Santa Fe

I said a prayer last night.
The words were all over the place,
just like I seem to be.
I promise I wasn't mad,
hopefully I didn't come across that way.
I said some things,
I said I believe.
Or at least I'm choosing to.
I asked if you believe in me.
Because it's become hard to believe in myself.
I couldn't even remember my name.
But that's not what I was praying about.
I want to be patient and at peace with life.
Honest and confident in my thoughts.
I've run out of words,
but I was told you know my heart.
There's a divide between my soul and my actions.
How do I bridge the two?
I was told you are the master of timing.
Maybe the pieces are just lining up.
But I fear that I'll just ignore when they do,
not because I don't believe,
but because I don't believe in myself.
I really wish I did.
I want patience and peace.
I want honesty and confidence.
I want to believe in...

# Hang With Me Here, I Can't Afford Therapy So I Write Instead

I overheard a lady talking. Two strangers having brunch next to me. And, frankly, it was none of my business. But she said something that sounded familiar to me. So, before I put my earbuds in, I listened in for a moment. Said something about the way she grew up. She didn't go into detail, but I could instantly connect the dots.

I grew up in the perfect family. That's what my parents told me. The illusion dropped eventually. If you had a problem, no you didn't. If you were feeling sad, try not feeling sad. I was the eldest, the golden child. They told me to speak my mind, but then everyone would realize I wasn't made of gold, but more of a copper alloy.

I've always had a lot on my mind. As a kid I would always tell people everything I was thinking, but then they told me to shut up. I don't know who they are, just the vague entity of the people around me. I felt embarrassed that I was inconveniencing people with the random thoughts in my head that really only made sense in the context of my head. Now I don't talk as much. Not in the same way, at least. Close friends will still say I'm always talking, but maybe that's because they never stop listening. Thank you for that, I get tired of only writing words for myself.

I'll never tell a kid they're mature for their age. The only difference between a well-spoken child and the class clown is one is afraid of being made a fool. Ask me how I know. I'm the smart one. I'm the mysterious one. I'm the quiet one. And emotional intelligence only gets you so far if you don't know how to speak your mind.

She keeps berating me for not eating anything. Says I'll fly away like a kite. Who's to say I haven't already? I'm not hungry. I'll eat later. You'll see me by the drink table. I always have a beverage in hand. And I'm always holding in my pee. Afraid if I step out for a moment, people will forget I was there to begin with. Do you want to know the truth? The part of the story I don't explain because I'm afraid it'll make me look bad. Whenever I'm around people, my body just shuts down. I'm too anxious to eat. Just the thought of food makes me begin to gag. I should really see someone about it, but I treat going to the doctor the same way I treat being around you. I'm nervous I won't like what you'll say to me, so I don't talk at all.

I grew up in the perfect family. That didn't last for long. Maybe I'm overthinking this all. The social anxiety, the obsession with people being proud of me. Maybe I can just blame it all on being homeschooled. It does seem to explain a lot. My parents taught me a lot of things, and I love and respect them in so many ways, but even they'll admit they never taught me how to have an honest conversation. And I'm not talking about lying, but how I only ever speak in half-truths. I learned to have integrity, but never how to be vulnerable with people. And they loved me for it. I don't know who they are, some amalgamation of all the people who've praised me for being a smart, young man.

She's pretty and funny. I would tell her, but what if she finds me weird? I have another friend who I want to hang out with. What if they're too busy for me? Lately, I've been feeling anxious, a little unwell at times. I'll never admit it though, because what would my family and friends think of me if they knew?

The lady sitting next to me said her family wasn't the type to have real conversations about things. Reality often breaks our illusion, after all. She never said anything about going to church, but I'm sure she grew up spending Sundays in a pew just like me. I still hold onto the notion that love is earned. I'm afraid to break the illusion, because then people won't want me around anymore. I fear that they will tell me to shut up, so I never give them a reason to. Why am I giving this insecurity of mine the satisfaction? Do I really think that constant half-truths are substantial? All anyone will ever see is half a person. And that's fifty percent too little for me. I want to make a fool of myself. I want to tell my friend I think she's cute, because she is. I want to stop caring what they will think.

Hey, guess what? My family was never perfect. I was never perfect. I'm not some mature, patient, talented prodigy. Behind the mask I'm a skinny, slightly self-obsessed, anxious writer. Hopelessly in love, hopeful in my beliefs. I'm just patient enough to teach a kid how to do a side kick, but I'm overeager for everything else. I'm well-spoken, well just you wait till you hear the things I decided not to say. I'm crazy. I like to think in the best ways. I've been so obsessed with this perfect illusion of myself, that I miss the things that make me human. I don't need to be made of gold for people to find worth in me.

To the lady next to me, I apologize for eavesdropping on your conversation. I hope you have a good rest of your day. And to the person reading this, I would apologize for bothering you with my rambling, but if you're still reading at this point, I probably shouldn't feel that sorry. Thank you for listening.

*I don't trust therapists.*
*What kind of human*
*profits from other*
*people's misery?*
*They're the lawyers of*
*the mind, the psychos of*
*the psyche.*

# Real Life Fan Fiction

Real life is boring and sad. It makes me quite mad.
So, I'm going to disregard the facts
and write things the way they should be.

In chapter one, I decide to pick up a guitar
and immediately nail each and every chord.
So, I write a song, and it sounds simply amazing.
Everyone loves it, and they ask me to write another.
"Just you wait," I say. "It's going to be great."

In chapter two, I ask the girl I like out on a date,
and she blushes at how charming I am.
So, we grab dinner and go for a walk.
At the end of the night she says, "We should do this again."
I smile and say to her, "Well, I'm free next Saturday."

In chapter three, I kick so much butt,
that everyone is like, "Hey, that kid is pretty darn good."
So, I take out a few black belts with my spinny kicks
and sweep a dude a foot taller than me off his feet
as I wink and say something clever and quippy.

In chapter four, I write another book,
and the pages start flying off the shelves.
So, I hold a book signing to meet all my adoring fans.
They tell me how much my words have impacted them,
and frankly, I find it all very touching.

In chapter five, I am talking with my girl,
and she tells me how she'll love me no matter what.
So, we talk about life and dreams for a while,
I tear up a bit as I realize she is always here for me,
and I tell her I'll never not be there for her.

In chapter six, I stub my toe on the corner of the couch,
and I try not to scream profanities into the ether.
So, I look the couch in the eyes, or cushions I guess,
and say to it, "How dare you betray me like this."
But it's okay, because every good story needs some drama.

In chapter seven, I celebrate a few birthdays
and start to notice things are changing.
So, I begin to wonder what comes next:
Kids, a house, mild fame, marriage, maybe a degree?
There's so much left to do, and I can't wait for it all.

In chapter eight, I am all grown up
and I think to myself I've had a pretty lucky life.
So, every day I look for ways to give back to the world.
My way of saying thanks for everything being so great.
It's my turn to make someone else smile.

In chapter nine, I have a little talk with God
as I wonder why my story went the way it did.
So, while waiting for a response, I begin thinking.
Was this the result of hard work or something more?
God or random chance? Maybe it was a mix of both.

In chapter ten, I sit down to write a little story
about change, love, creativity, inspiration, and family.
So, I open a new tab on my computer screen.
I type a few words, then shake my head and erase them.
I do this for a couple hours, unable to write anything.

Eventually, I just smile and close my computer.
I walk back into the living room,
where my favorite people are waiting for me.
We eat dinner together and go for a walk around town.
In the end I know there's no story I could write
that would ever be better than real life.

# Keep Fighting

Life has this funny habit of just when you think you have it all figured out, wreaking everything with a storm. Even if it's the middle of November. The things I thought I knew make no sense to me now. I said I was going to leave it all behind, all the pain, all the nonsense, but I paused once I stepped my right foot out the door. I've been walking in all directions, and I don't understand what it means. I'm not even sure who I am anymore, and I mean that in a more literal sense than you may realize. Things have been crazy, when are they not? All year I've been chasing something shiny, disregarding where it's led me. Distracted by something pretty in more ways than one.

I worked myself till I was sick. Confronted by a cold front, now I'm wearing multiple layers and still shaking. Sniffling while I write, overheating while I teach. I used to sleep just fine, but anymore I can't make it through the night in one go. I wonder if I would be happier if I knew less about myself. They say ignorance is bliss but look where ignorance got us. I just turned on the news to see that our leaders are assembling a super team of the worst people you know. And I have to just keep going, act like that's okay. Pretend to be normal.

I could leave. Why bother fighting a fight you'll only lose? I can't change the people I'm not, and I won't become the person I'm not. Life has this funny habit of contradicting itself with a rhyme. Like in the funny way I always think I'm running out of time. The closer I get to running away, the more I want to stay and fight. I can never just make up my mind. But I've also never felt so happy in a place I swear I'm trapped in.

Every time I pray I walk right back over my own words, then try to apologize for the constant rambling. Why do I spend so much time saying sorry for being who I am? I said I was going to leave it all behind, but I still haven't. And honestly, I don't want to. Instead, I want to take the best parts of life and hold them as close as possible. Feel their warmth even when it gets cold. I won't apologize for that. Things have been crazy, we all know that much, but so what? I'm not going to let that stop me from believing in life, I only get one after all. Just the same, I believe in you. And I want to believe that you love me too.

I've always told my kids that when you get knocked down you have to stand back up. When the bullies punch you in the face you punch them back. When life takes you down you can't just stay on the ground. Hey kid, we're about to have to stand back up a lot. We're going to get knocked down again and again and again. It's starting to feel like I should just lie down and take it. Just accept fate. But no. I've never been one to back down or run away. Because I'm a fighter. And I'm going to keep fighting. Even when I'm bruised and sore, I'm going to keep fighting. Even when it hurts to get out of bed, I'm going to keep going. Because that's what I do. I keep fighting.

Nothing and no one are going to stop me from living life. No villain will keep me down. No fear is going to stop me from falling in love. No friend will prevent me from being honest. And I truly do believe, I believe that no storm will ever stop me.

# Silvia

"For a moment I close my eyes and start to strum the strings of my guitar. It's one of those moments when you can feel the music guide you. It's drawing out every last drop of blood in your heart and every tear you've been storing up."

*For every friend I've known,*
*past, present, or future.*
*I hope I don't forget about you.*
*I pray I won't ever stop loving you.*

# Silvia

*Introduction*

My friend Silvia and I go to school together,
I see her every day and she smiles like the sun.
But right now it's overcast, and her smile's gone.
Silvia, why aren't you laughing?
You seem a bit off today, is everything okay?
We used to go over to your house and play.
Why don't you want to hangout anymore?
Silvia, can I come over today?
You just say it'd be better if I didn't.
Why is that? Did I do something wrong?
You keep telling me no, it's not my fault.
I don't know if I believe you.

*Chapter 1: Kids*

Can't we still be friends?
You seem so engulfed in your world;
have you forgotten about me?
What did I do to deserve this from you?
What is it that you aren't telling me?
You're my best friend.
I don't want that to end.
I'm just trying to be a kid.
I never asked for this.

*Chorus*

Silvia, why do you wear your jacket in the summer?
Your makeup takes up the space on your face
where you've always been beautiful to me.
You used to be the light in my life
but now you keep your distance.
Silvia, you always carry a black diary
that the world isn't allowed to see inside of.
You stare out the window,
pale and scared; your spirit stolen from you.
There I am sitting next to you, a world away,
and I don't notice the tear in the corner of your eye.
And for that, I'm so sorry.

*Chapter 2: Trust*

You seem nervous, like every day.
I guess I know what that's like.
It seemed like there was something
you wanted to tell me. But you didn't.
Silvia, why don't you trust me?
I trust you. You're the smartest person I know.
Why do people keep their problems to themselves?
Maybe you think I don't deserve to be burdened
by a so-called 'waste of space' like you.
Maybe I just wish I could've been a better friend.

*Chapter 3: Poetry*

You started writing poetry. Gross.
You told me it was a way to feel free,
I didn't believe you.
I'd rather write a script for a movie.
You snickered at me and said
I should learn how to write about who I am,
instead of trying to be who I can never be.
I still think about that.

*Chapter 4: Quiet*

Damn, Silvia. You've gotten so pretty.
Which might be why I was so taken aback
when you said you hated the way you look.
It made me think, what makes you think that?
I don't care if the other kids call you a bitch.
They're just jealous. I overhear everything they say.
She's the sexy and quiet girl dressed in black.
They say she's unapproachable.
They don't know you like I do.
All I see from you is a caring person.
When no one is watching, you're so desperately sweet.
You want everyone to feel welcome and safe;
to save them from feeling the way you do.

*Chapter 5: Irony*

Do you remember when you
asked me what Heaven must be like?
You said Hell doesn't scare you
because why would a loving father
make his daughter live in pain.
The irony completely lost on me.

*Chorus*

Silvia, why do you wear your jacket in the summer?
Your makeup takes up the space on your face
where you've always been beautiful to me.
You used to be the light in my life
but now you keep your distance.
Silvia, you always carry a black diary
that the world isn't allowed to see inside of.
You stare out the window,
pale and scared; your spirit stolen from you.
There I am sitting next to you, a world away,
and I don't notice the tear in the corner of your eye.
And for that, I'm so sorry.

*Chapter 6: Fine*

Sixteen already, we're getting older every day.
Did you have a good birthday?
You said it was 'fine.' Thanks for lying.
You're always 'fine,' what really happened last night?
You know better than I do, so you wouldn't tell me.
If I had known, there's no telling what I would've said.
So, I let it be, went back to trying to be the best friend
I could be at the time. Some days I fear it wasn't enough.

*Chapter 7: Attention*

I wish I complimented you more.
You deserved to know how highly I thought of you.
I was so worried about getting attention
from the new craze of the week,
girls who didn't give a shit about me.
You never could see the prettiness in your smile,
because people would use you up.
The audacity they had to tell you to shut up.

*Chapter 8: Tattoo*

Silvia and her black diary.
She wrote everything in that thing.
"The world can't harm you when
you're lost in ink," she would say.
Silvia told me she would get a tattoo
of her favorite poem on her arm one day.
I asked her what she thought would hurt more,
the needle or being forced to read poetry
every time she looked at her arm.
She thought about it then began to laugh,
a laugh that seemed to ease something inside of her.
After she caught her breath she told me,
"You always make me laugh. Thank you."
I don't know what about what I said was so funny,
but I do know I'd do anything to make you laugh.

*Chapter 9: Fantasy*
Silvia asked me if God is real,
then why did he forget about her.
Heaven is like that distant dream,
a fantasy of make-believe.
She said, "Why would I believe in God,
if he doesn't believe in me?"

*Chorus*
Silvia, why do you wear your jacket in the summer?
Your makeup takes up the space on your face
where you've always been beautiful to me.
You used to be the light in my life
but now you keep your distance.
Silvia, you always carry a black diary
that the world isn't allowed to see inside of.
You stare out the window,
pale and scared; your spirit stolen from you.
There I am sitting next to you, a world away,
and I don't notice the tear in the corner of your eye.
And for that, I'm so sorry.

*Chapter 10: Bedroom*
In high school, you called me one night.
You were crying on the floor of your bedroom
and I didn't know what to say to comfort you.
Silvia, why did you call me?
I still lay awake at night wondering why me.
When I said, "I love you," the words meant nothing.
You wouldn't tell me why those
three words had lost all meaning.
To you, they sound like a lie.
I promise you this: I've never lied to you.
And my eye twitches at the thought of those who would.

*Chapter 11: Lake*

We were by the lake with our friends
when I got a peak underneath your life.
You went for swim in just a t-shirt and my heart broke
at the sight of the scars and tattered remains.
I'm still not sure I've ever seen a young woman
as brave and confident as you were on that day.
You brushed off the dread and smiled the whole time.
It was that new smile I've gotten used to.
You wanted everyone to think you were happy.
If I was a bit smarter I would've known you weren't.

*Chapter 12: Evil*

Do you still have trouble sleeping at night?
How do you find comfort when nightmares
fill the space where you're supposed to dream?
And yet, you tell me you sleep in just to forget it all.
I don't see you on Sundays anymore.
The spot next to me is an empty pew.
During the sermon, what you told me rings through.
"Where is God in all the pain?"
"What is Heaven, if evil is all we know?"

*Chapter 13: Coffee*

We got our jobs and clubs, so we started talking less.
I guess that's natural. I try not to think about it, but alas.
Time for me to grow up, time to mature.
You unwillingly beat me to that years ago.
Hey, let's grab coffee Tuesday.
I'll miss you when we graduate,
even if it feels like I hardly know you anymore.

## *Chapter 14: Homecoming*

It was homecoming night when you walked by.
The girl I had liked dancing with some guy.
I was standing by the punch table trying not to cry.
"I'm guessing she said no?" you asked.
"Um, actually, I didn't ask her out.
Turns out she already has a boyfriend."
"That sucks," Silvia replied.
"Just remember, your worth isn't determined
by those who don't want you.
Or at least that's what I keep trying to remind myself.
And hey, at least you know I love you."

*(Silvia, I love you too)*
How long will you live with the scars?
The ones I never knew you had.
You were just trying to be a kid.
You never asked for this.
*(I hope you're okay)*
How long will you live with a broken heart?
The body mistreated and abused.
The arms bloodied and tear-soaked.
The scars etched into your heart.
*(Please be okay)*

She smiled at me and asked,
"Do you still wanna dance?"

## *Bridge*

Silvia, why do you wear your jacket in the summer?
Why - when you are so smart - can't you love yourself?
Can't we just keep dancing?
Silvia, why do you carry that black diary?

*Chapter 15: Graduation*
Congrats on graduating early,
like I said, you were always the smart one.
I heard you were quick to move away.
Away from the pain you knew.
They asked me to help clean out your locker
and I found your black diary.
Don't hate me when I tell you I took it.
I opened it and read it.
. . .
Now I know why you aren't scared of Hell.

*Epilogue*
Silvia, I hope you're doing okay.
We haven't talked for a couple years,
I hope college is going well for you.
The other day I saw a picture of you online,
the one with the new haircut
and a pretty girl next to you.
You looked happy; I hope it was real.
Every day I wish I could be as
strong as half the person you are.
But honestly, I'm not sure I ever will.
I was thinking about you the other day
and what I read in that black diary of yours.
When you were sitting next to me, a world away,
I never noticed the tear in the corner of your eye.
And for that, I'm so sorry.

*Silvia, I'm so sorry.*

# Imaginary Friends

## chapter i

# a chicken quesadilla with a root beer to drink

i have been trying to avoid the obvious.
there are some days where i hit a curb
while driving and just start crying.
i'll order lunch while out with friends
then barely touch the food on my plate.
i smile at all the right jokes
before my eyes fall out of focus,
the room begins to shift and change.
everything around me feels real,
but i feel imaginary.

# Lunch With Soj

I sit at a table at that local Mexican place,
waiting patiently for you to arrive.
My plate sitting in front of me,
a book I wrote lying to the side.
I take another sip of my soda,
close my eyes and take a deep breath.

Hey Soj, can we talk?
Maybe for a bit over lunch.
I talked with God, he said to talk with you.
My friend, you've been on my mind,
a quite of bit, I might say.

I open my eyes, see you smiling across the table.
*"Hey man, how's it been going?"*
Oh y'know, the typical. This and that, and whatnot.
But I've been doing good.
And I really think I mean it this time.
*"I'm glad. It's nice to see you looking happy again."*
Thanks, it hasn't always been easy,
but I don't think I would have had it any other way.

*"So, tell me, how's the book coming along?"*
It's done. Here, I brought a copy of it with me.
Hopefully the title isn't too on the nose.
I took some of your notes and edits into account,
and I'll say I'm pretty happy with how it turned out.
It's not exactly what I originally planned,
but life never is, is it?
*"Mind if I flip through?"*
Not at all. You can even keep it if you'd like.

*"Have you talked with any of the others recently?"*
No, not really. Just you, here and there.
I do miss them, but I think it was for the best.
I've made some really amazing friends in the past year.
And I'm really happy to have those people in my life.
*"That's awesome, man. I think we all knew that*
*eventually we would need to go our separate ways."*
Yeah. You know I'll always love you and Jenna, Silvia too,
but it was time for us to go and be our own people.
Make friends of our own. Real ones for once.

*"I've been meaning to ask, how's your leg healing?"*
It's been getting better. Still hurts some days,
but with each week that goes by it hurts a little less.
I did decide to put the gloves down for a while.
I'll always be a fighter, but I've learned it's okay to rest too.
*"I can't blame you. I've never seen a punch*
*land as hard as the ones he threw your way."*
You're telling me. I can still feel the bruises when I shower.
But hey, I'm still breathing. That's what matters the most.

*"I really mean it, I'm glad to see you smiling.*
*It's never easy for me to see you looking down."*
Thank you. I wouldn't be here without you.
I'd still be lying on the gravel after a fight.
Still crying in the shower at night.
I've spent a lot of time mythologizing myself.
Trying to understand why I am this way.
The poetry and songs keep me alive.
But Soj, I could never imagine
something better than this.
I pass him a folded up picture.
*"Sounds like you've had a wonderful time."*
*"I'm happy for you, Joshua."*

## Dusty Bookshelf

I spend my morning cleaning,
looking for the inspiration to write.
Find a book with my words on the bookshelf.
I read it, looking for a new idea.
Only could find old thoughts inside.

Found a black diary amongst the dust.
I wipe the leather clean,
open the pages with a creak.
I skip around, read a few poems inside.
Stories left behind, though the stories aren't mine.
Some good, some bad, all important.
The doodles, the little drawings,
my eyes swelling the further I read.

A picture taped to a notebook page.
High school friends by the lake.
The image different in my memory.
I stand there, smiling awkwardly.
I chuckle, about right for me.
There's one person missing,
she's holding the camera,
telling me to smile normally.
Her words written in a poem below.

*"I fear I'm imaginary.*
*That my friends can't really see me.*
*I don't want to keep the feeling that I need to be hiding.*
*Let these be the words that free me."*

I wipe the tears from my eyes.
The dust must've got to me.
Grab my wallet, keys, and computer bag.
I know what I'm going to write about today.

# Jacket Weather

It's gotten cold out again.
Spent the year dreaming and making friends.
Missing the old ones.
Silvia, I think I understand now.
Why you wore your jacket in the summertime.

It's gotten cold out again.
Spent the year fighting and falling in love.
Trying to love who I am.
Silvia, I think I understand now.
Why you stared out that window for so long.

It's gotten cold out again.
Spent the year walking and going out late.
Writing stories line by line.
Silvia, I think I understand now.
Why you always carried that black diary around.

I bundled up last night.
Took a walk around the neighborhood.
Silvia, here's my story.

# Nineteen

Who do you call when
you're nineteen and all alone?
Something to say, nowhere to go.
Who do you call then?

Trying to write a song without a melody.
Trying to perfect a life that hasn't started.
Why can't I start something without
having to know what the end will be?
Perfectionism will be the end of me.

A boy living in his car more than home.
A girl crippled by fear and anxiety.
They're still kids trying to be something more.

I re-question all my queries daily,
make up words to describe feelings.
Yet I only wear makeup on the days
I know no one will see me.
What kind of clown only dresses up
on their days away from the circus?
I want to be liked, possibly loved.
Be seen as pretty, possibly worthy.
But I won't let myself be seen at all.

Who do you call when
you're nineteen and all alone?
Something to say, nowhere to go.
Who do you call then?

I've given names to the voices in my head.
Started assigning personality to my thoughts.
There are days when I need to talk with someone,
but I don't wish to bother anyone with my problems.
I'll talk to myself, I'll argue with the voices,
anything to avoid prayer and or therapy.
Or just an honest conversation outside the shower.

A boy predicting a future he hasn't seen.
A girl looking for love, swiping left instead.
They're still kids trying to be something more.

Who do you call when
you're nineteen and all alone?
Something to say, nowhere to go.
Who do you call then?

A boy staying inside on a Saturday night.
A girl losing touch with her sense of self.
They're still kids trying to be something more.

Who do you call when
you're nineteen and all alone?
Who do you call when
you don't have your phone?
Don't convince yourself you're
at your best when you're on your own.
Who do you call on your hardest days?
Something to say, nowhere to go.
Who do you call then?

# Friday Night Blues

Let it all go, don't let it get to you.
The stress and expectations build,
but you do it for the love of the game.
Let it all go, don't let it get to you.
Now you can be beautiful.

By yourself again tonight.
Honey, eat something. You're looking skinny.
You play dress up just to go on a walk.
Swipe a few times. Check your empty inbox.
Honey, turn the TV off. Read a book.
Let yourself be happy for a moment,
before the world returns to you.
Why don't you let it all go? You let it get to you.
Tomorrow you'll still be beautiful.

They're expecting you to smile, girl.
Ripped from your bed, ripped from your world,
but they need you to be friendly still.
And you know you want to.
But you can't let it all go. It got away from you.
You no longer feel beautiful.

Hold on. The same heart still beats.
I know it's not always ideal.
You have to take the highs with the lows.
Let it all go, don't let it get to you.
They'll see how you're beautiful.

# Imaginary Girl

When I dream, I see her silhouette dancing
in the reflection of store windows.
A sketch of lines drawn to perfection.
Her figure is precisely gorgeous,
from each curve to each color,
and when I look down at my hands
I figure she'll never see me.

Hair like silk, glowing under streetlights.
So gorgeous in her crop top and swing skirt.
Walks like she's dancing, a voice like an angel,
hear her singing in my car at night.

I don't know who you are.
All I know is you're beautiful.
I don't even know who I am.
But you know the best in me.
If I could glance at the night sky
and pray a single wish to the stars,
they'd hear me say I want to be like you.

She's so pretty, like no one else ever could be.
Strong enough to not collapse under the insecurities.
Her smile shining with grace and patience.
Most of all she loves herself.
Loves her every curve and color,
and when she looks down at her hands
all she sees is something beautiful.

When I watch the reflections in store windows,
she's the girl I dream of seeing.

# The Need to Apologize II

Dear Jenna, I feel the need to apologize.
I can't even look you in the eyes.
I'm conflicted all the fucking time.
I knew who I was until I didn't.
It must be exhausting to deal with me.
Can't make a choice to save my life.
I made so much progress, so why am I not happy?
You're so pretty, we both know I'm not.

Dear Joshua, are you actually sorry?
I think you're avoiding me cause you're ashamed of me.
Bitch, I read your last book.
Are those not the words you wrote?
I'm tired of not knowing where we stand.
Just stop choosing to live in uncertainty,
and stop chasing happiness like it's an accomplishment.
I may be pretty, but I say I'm just being true to me.

Jenna, what do you think?
Which one of us is the imaginary one? You or me?
I would never admit it, but I don't really like myself.
There's this deeply rooted sense of self-loathing in me.

Joshua, I think you know what I think.
Life is only imaginary as you make it out to be.
I understand the feeling, but listen to me please,
hating yourself is no way to live your life.

Dear Jenna, I'm in love with a girl I shouldn't be.
Can't make these feelings go away no matter
how hard I try. Though I've barely tried.
Jenna, I don't even know what I'm writing about.
At every corner, I take a different turn.
Is this what it feels like to be lost?
I just wish I knew the correct way to go,
but Jenna, what if that is the way away from you?

Dear Joshua, every girl I love is one I shouldn't.
Don't force yourself to change the way you feel,
but please, I mean it, remember you deserve love too.
Joshua, this is your story, I can't change it for you.
But what is the problem with something different?
Maybe growing up is realizing you're not that smart.
I don't know how tomorrow will go,
but Joshua, I'm still excited for what it will bring.

Dear Jenna, we don't talk as much anymore, why is that?
You were the one who showed me how to live life.
I don't want to hurt you. You deserve the world.
You deserve better than a mess like me.
Jenna, you're beautiful.
I'm sorry if I don't say it enough.

Dear Joshua, it's not like I'm that hard to get a hold of.
Why won't you be honest with me?
Don't give me some shit about just looking out for me.
You deserve to see yourself like I see you.
Joshua, you're beautiful.
I'm sorry if you don't realize that.

# My Business

Another bruise. Another paycheck.
Though I'm not in it for the money.
Don't tell my mom.
I wouldn't want her to worry.

I leave work on Friday night,
wave goodbye to the last kid in sight.
Pack my punching gloves,
stick my mouthpiece in my pocket.
I drive to a house on the east side of town.
There are cars parked around the block,
I walk around the back,
knock on a rickety side door.
A man stands tall in my way.
He asks me what my business is.

My business, you ask?
I'm the toy you pay only to break.
I'm the one who cleans blood with teeth.
I hear the cheers while my ears ring.
I'm the one who makes the sick sing.
You smile at the pain of my sin.
So, I'll only ask one more time:
You gonna let me in?

I sit in the corner, staring into the distance.
The crowd places their money at the feet of vermin.
Drunkards hoist another lukewarm beer.
Degenerates spit the vile they swear.
Another man sits in the corner opposite of mine.
I don't know him, we've only spoken once,
yet he's my closest friend here.
The only other one here with a purpose.

I step into the ring.
Tried to find the thrill in comfort,
found I only feel alive when I fight.
I never play the same, I just love the game.
It always ends in pain, for that they call me insane.
They tout my losing streak, one win for every three losses.
But I always keep it close,
lose by points in the waning seconds.
And isn't that why they pay me so well?
They don't want a winner, just a show.

We trade blows. He tries to take my legs.
Better than you have tried and failed.
Spit on who I am. I'll stand my ground.
I weave under, grab by the waist, drop to the floor.
I keep pressure, fight for a lock, so many times I had it all.
You grab hold, flip me, I'm too small to beat the call.
Seconds left, you drop an elbow to my face.
Grab my collar, I turn pale, the crowd yells for me to give in.
They must not know me very well.
I mutter a prayer between deep breaths.
The bell beckons her victim. They call it by points.
I stand up, blood dripping from the face.
You look exhausted. I just look your way.
I should have lost. I usually do.
They say I won. I say I survived.

When my family ask where I've been,
I'll tell them that's my business.
I'm the toy you pay only to break.
I'm the one who cleans blood with teeth.
I hear the cheers while my ears ring.
I'm the one who makes the sick sing.
You smile at the pain of my sin.
And I don't care if I stand victorious:
Just know I'll always stand again.

# Below Freezing

It's finally too cold for me to go for an evening stroll.
I was too stubborn to stay inside,
but the winter wind finally got to me.
I don't want to get out of bed in the morning,
but I equally hate staying there with my thoughts.
I'll waste all day on my couch watching YouTube,
constantly refreshing the TV for a new episode,
anything to distract me from my latest depressive episode.
I have no inspiration, nothing interesting to write about.
The notes app on my phone is full of half-baked ideas
and a long rambling monologue
that should not be considered poetry
but an attempt at reasoning with one's inner dread.
People ask me, 'How are you doing?'
If I bother to answer at all, I hesitantly say okay.
And I'll pretend to be fine. And some days I am.
I'll keep myself stimulated and busy,
distracted by productive things.
I can put on a smile for a bit,
wear multiple jackets to my car,
but that doesn't change the fact
that it's still so cold.

# Emergency Vehicles

Flu cases are on the rise.
Schools are closing,
businesses are hurting.
January isn't even over and our country has
already experienced three separate tragedies.
They said the price of eggs would go down,
it immediately went up instead.
I've heard stories from people I know
about young children passing away.
Everywhere I look I see people struggling.
People kicked out of their country.
People mourning the loss of loved ones.
People barely making ends meet.
And me, my problems seem small in comparison,
yet I've been left frozen from multiple panic attacks.
*What's going on?*

I have seen an unusually high amount
of emergency vehicles on the road lately.
I hope everyone is okay.

chapter ii

# writing poems is the most pretentions form of disassociation

you ever feel sad for no reason at all?
i'm here, physically,
my thoughts couldn't be further away.
what you see isn't real.
a hollow breath in my laugh,
the reflection in the mirror is empty,
the soul behind these eyes hidden from you.
every chance i get,
i lose myself to poetry.
any distraction, any way to reason with this.
you ever feel sad for any reason at all?

# Depression Poetry

*Hey Joshua, we need to talk.*

About what?

*Your new book. You can't publish this.*
*This isn't anything,*
*it's just a bunch of incoherent babble.*

What do you mean?
I think this is some of my best writing yet.

*No you don't. You oh-so-clearly don't.*
*Joshua, I think you've blurred the line*
*between what counts as poetry and*
*what is just journaling your thoughts.*
*This isn't art. Far from it.*

And who are you to make that distinction?
The best stories are inspired by real life.
I take my own experiences and craft
them into wonderful, written prose.

*Yeah, but this isn't that.*
*We're not talking about Silvia here.*
*This isn't about that girl you saw in November.*
*This is coping. You're just trying to survive.*
*It's obvious that you haven't been doing okay.*
*And you think that if you just write about it*
*then it'll all have been worth it.*
*This is depression poetry.*

Soj, shut up.
I'm fine. I'm a great writer. I'm not depressed.
This is just the next chapter in my story.
I take my life and create art with it.
That's what I do, okay.
It doesn't matter what happens,
cause it's my job to turn it into something worth telling.
I'm fine. I'm perfectly fine.
I just had one bad day, don't we all.
So, just shut up.

*Don't try to convince me or anyone*
*that you wrote all this in one day.*
*How many times did you rewrite that song?*
*You know the one I'm talking about.*
*Do you think that if you never finish writing it*
*then it means you never have to say goodbye?*
*It's okay. It's okay to not always be okay.*
*But please don't fool yourself that you are.*
*I think you're right when you say you can really write.*
*You like to take something sad,*
*use music to make it seem a little less bad.*
*But please admit to yourself that these poems*
*were never meant to be your next great book.*
*They're just your way of coming to terms*
*with the harder parts of life.*
*And that's okay. Things will be okay.*

But Soj...
...what if they're not?

# Creative Kid

They called me creative when I was kid.
I'd tell a story whenever I saw the chance.
It felt like every interest I had
made me interesting back then.
What happened over the past
twenty years to change that?
Went from a kid with aspirations to write a movie
to a gloomy poet who hasn't made a sale in months.
They say you have all the potential when you're little
but are let down if you don't use it their way.
It was cute for a while to watch me write down
the imaginary conversations I had in my head,
now they say their concerned for me.
People keep asking me if I'm okay, and the scariest part
of that is I don't know if those people are even real
or just some distant echo inside of me,
desperately trying to escape onto these pages.
Latching onto the story like some parasite.
At what point does the narrative I created
start controlling me instead?
I used to write fantasy and sci-fi, I drew comics,
now I put content warnings in front of poetry.
I used to feel free when I finished a story,
now the walls of this book are closing in on me.
I'm not done yet, just give me another month,
I promise you this story will have a happy ending.
I just haven't found it yet. But I will. I have to.
Because the lines between reality and my imagination
are increasingly blurred in my head.
And it's my creativity that's haunting me.

# Some Other Day

I get it, we're both busy.
We can be friends again on some other day.

I use the same excuse as I always do:
I told you I forgot to text again.
And there's some truth in that.
But what's worse, that I lied or forgot about you?
I only reach out when I want something.
You don't even do that.
But that's alright, cause times have been crazy, huh?
And there I go with another excuse.

I get it, we're both busy.
I have work, you have stuff.
I don't know what, but it's always something.
We can be friends again on some other day.

I'll be honest. I know people drift apart with time,
I just never thought we would.
We're both busy, but when something is important to you,
you make time for it. So, what's that say about us?
We can be friends again on some other day,
but I've changed. And you're not exactly the same.
The Venn diagram of our lives is just two circles.
We have friends of our own.
All these exciting, new dreams.
I hate to admit it, but when I need advice
you're no longer the person I find.

I get it, we're both busy.
We both have so many stories to tell,
but those stories will be told differently.
It's okay, we can be friends again on some other day.

# Problems

Dear Silvia,
my problems seem small compared to yours,
but I want to ask for some advice regardless.
How did you do it?
How did you make it through the day?
I feel so tired all the time.
I know I'm not okay.
Maybe I should just run away too.
How did you convince yourself things would get better?
How did you get out of bed in the morning?
Because I don't want to most days.
Did your black diary help you process things?
I'm not sure my poetry is having the same effect.
I sat in my car last night, crying.
It took the rest of the evening just to clear my mind.
How did you do it?
How did you learn to keep going?

I think of something you told me once:
*"I don't want to be alone right now.*
*Can you just stay here a little longer?"*
I did. I was just trying to be a good friend,
even if I didn't understand the problem.
I just need a friend.
I've been trying really hard to love myself.
And I do. But it doesn't feel like enough.
I need someone like you.
Just stay by my side.

My problems seem small in comparison,
but you once told me everyone has the right to be sad.
Silvia, do you see the tear in the corner of my eye?

# Dead Kitten

Dead kitten on the road.
Blood spread by the head.
Met a death where
rubber met gravel stone.

Dead kitten on the road.
Too small to take on life alone.
Lying still while cars go on.
No reason to stop for what's already gone.

Dead kitten on the road.
Itty-bitty kitty made flat.
No pity from the city.
Victim of this mechanical ditty.

Dead kitten on the road.
Blood spread by the head.
So young, so small,
there's no mercy in this world.

# Cloudy Eye

My next fight is tonight.
They tell me don't do it.
He'll kill you they say.
But for all the shit I talk,
I'm not the type to run away.

The lights flash and strobe.
Cheers of mockery ring around.
The hungry lion roars for her meal.

Behind a wall of fog, he finally steps out.
His silhouette blinds me like a light in the mirror.
I can't get a good read on him.
There's a mask over his face.
His ragged hair hides his humanity.
I can tell by the way he walks
that this is more than business.
To him this fight is personal.
Every muscle of his punches are filled with hate.

I meet him in the ring.
His eyes are cloudy, unrecognizable.
I stare him down.
A chill creeps down my spine.
Every bone in my body turns.
Behind his hazy gaze there's nothing,
my own soul draining in the reflection.
The silence screams at me.
I know I'm not strong enough, I never really was.
Every fear I've ever had come to a boil,
filling my head like poison.

I take a deep breath,
try to remember who I am.
We tap gloves.
I'm shaking, no more than usual.
My guard is up. My feet planted.
The ref counts down.

*(Ladies and gentlemen!)*
What are you doing?
*(Welcome to our main event!)*
You don't belong here.
*(The fight will start on my call!)*
They all see right through you.
*(5...)*
They see that you're weak.
*(4...)*
You know it. Everyone knows it.
*(3...)*
Your friends will all leave you.
*(2...)*
Everyone you love hates you.
*(1...)*
You're just a sad, sorry, little kid.
*(Fight!)*

I throw a jab. I'm met with a slip and counter,
a fist that connects immediately.
Less than ten seconds in,
I fall to the floor with a thud.

# Hospital Bed

Fluorescent light shines from the sky.
No pain, too many drugs. I just feel numb.
A body on the gurney, my soul far from here.

They say my heart stopped for a moment,
but my lungs were too stubborn to quit breathing.
I talk to my mom over the phone,
tell her I nearly died, won't tell her why.
The blood didn't show the whole story.
You thought you could prove them all wrong.
Hey kid, you proved nothing!

I won't let them see how broken I am.
Woke with a smile, hiding the pain underneath.
Laughed for a while, there was nothing there.
It could takes days, some say months before I'll be okay.
The scars will stay as long as I let them stay.

It wasn't the collision that hurt
but what happened when I fell to the floor.
The jeers and cries echo in my head,
calling me pathetic, saying get up you pansy.
You failure of a someone. You loser.
You were right to say you're not enough.
Hey kid, you'll never be!

I can't let them know how broken I am.
Woke with a smile, lied about my wellbeing.
Laughed in denial, there was nothing there.
It could takes days, some say months before I'll be okay.
The scars will stay as long as I let them stay.

# The Definition Of

It's insanity. To do this over and over.
Expect my life to change for the better.

Ran out of breath, didn't know I could.
Got knocked down and didn't get back up.
Was injured for months, but I love the pain.
Roll with the punches, I'll roll into a ball.
Your words cut deeper than my knife can.
You keep the blood on your tongue
while mine drips to the cement.

Is it supposed to get harder each time?
I don't want to fight anymore.
First time I've said that in my life.
Again and again, it's always the same.
I get my hopes up, I put up my best lies,
but I'm not falling in love, just falling down.

*I can't. Not again. I can't. Not again. I can't.*
I worked so hard. I made so much progress.
*Not again. I can't. Not again. I can't. Not again.*
Only for the results to be the same as always.
*I can't. Not again. I can't. Not again. I can't.*
As I eye the horizon, the fear settles in the sky.
*Not again. I can't. Not again. I can't. Not again.*
Why do I keep doing this to myself?

# Dead on Arrival

I remember getting out my computer on the way back. I just wanted to do what I always do. No matter how I feel–whether I'm happy, sad, nostalgic, angry, in love, depressed–I just want to write. Put those feelings on paper. Or in this case, a word doc on my hard drive.

I had my earbuds in, listening to The Narcissist Cookbook and Rilo Kiley till I ran out of songs to play. I tried to write a new tune as the sun blinded me from the eastern sky. I distracted myself with new book ideas that I haven't touched since. I kept eyeing a file I had saved away; all the title said was *sap.* I hovered my mouse key over before moving it away.

Got a latte from a gas station. Tried to take a nap. Probably should have swapped the order on those two. For a while I just watched out the window. I can't entirely explain what was going through my mind at that moment. I don't know if I can think of a day where my thoughts were more at odds with one another than that day. I've never felt more confident in the way I felt, and I've never felt more unsure of how to say it.

I eventually reopened my computer. I clicked on that file and began writing a song. I've since rewritten it multiple times, with every revision the story stays the same. I wanted to include that song in this book but thought better of it. It's still not done. I'm not done rewriting it, and I won't be until I admit why I won't let myself finish it. Because when I put the pen down I'll have to face the fact that I won't ever find the final verse I've been looking for. This song, since the day I first started writing it, has been the place I could escape to when I needed to process these complicated feelings in my head. So, every once in a while I'll click copy and paste and start it anew. A new demo, a different draft, the same chorus every time.

Once it got dark out I stepped outside. It was freezing cold. I had something to say, but I just walked away instead. Threw my computer bag into my car. I can't remember if I cried, I do remember the prayer I said. I replayed memories like they were episodes of my favorite TV show. I replayed the same music I had been listening to all day, trying to find some hidden message in their melodies. I was already thinking of new lyrics to the song I had written only hours earlier. Maybe someday I'll finally finish writing it.

# Staring Out the Window

Writing time turns into
staring out the window time.
Should be writing, but I'm just thinking.
At least I keep on theme
by keeping these words to myself.
I have journal entries to finish.
I know exactly what to say,
but the words aren't coming to me.
There are titles given to this feeling.
Writer's block. Burnout. Depression.
I don't know which one fits best.
Maybe they all do.
Where has my love for the craft gone?
Did it disappear when she did?

Writing time turns into
staring out the window time.
Imagining conversations with friends.
Conversations that I'll never have,
though I probably should.
I'll be okay. I promise I will be.
I'll be okay. I just wish I could find
the words to prove so.

# The Star That Crystallized

Moonlight. Romanticizing depression.
Cut the sky with a butter knife.
Broken jewelry. Hair ties, pity lies.
Questioning your own heartbeat.
Oh, the wonders of being young.

A jacket lying idle. Dust on the mantle.
Lipstick left with the cap still on.
Everything is fine. Keep the lid closed.
The prettiest nights are kept quiet.
The longest walks end in weeping.
When you feel weak, even the air feels heavy.
Rather fight to be alive than feel nothing inside.

Oh, little one, why are you so sad?
Oh, my friend, why do you let the bad
be colored with a rose-bled sense of what you had.
One day all this will fade, but you'll stay.

They'll see a boy who stayed strong.
They'll see a son who made his mom proud.
They'll see a friend who always cared.
They'll see a girl who never backed down.
They'll see a kid with hearts in their eye.
They'll see a promise kept alive.
They'll see that you're beautiful.
They'll see that you're kind.
They'll see you making the most of this life.

In the future this teardrop will crystallize
and become a star, shining in your smile.

# this song is a coping mechanism

What am I supposed to do when writing doesn't work as a coping mechanism? I've yet to find any words that can stop this pain in my chest. I've been trying to not admit this, but I'm not doing well. And there are no words I can write that are just going to make this feeling go away. So, I'm stuck searching for something new, a new way to cope, a better way to cope, anything at all that will help me forget the memories in my mind.

𝄞♪♫♪♫♪

Oh-hmm-oh-hmm. Don't want to get out of bed.
Oh-hmm-oh-hmm. Not sure what to write about anymore.
Oh-hmm-oh-hmm. I can smile, but I'm barely hanging on.
Oh-hmm-oh-hmm. What now? Where do I go from here?

How do people avoid their brain? The vices they turn to turn into mechanisms of their failing emotional state. Food and wine, prayer and religion, disassociation from real life. How long before I replace constant disassociation with functional alcoholism as a coping mechanism? Drink just enough to trick myself into thinking that I'm not a complete mess, wake up feeling the consequences of that, but at least it'll be my head hurting instead of my heart. You can cure a headache with medicine and rest, but a broken heart can't be so easily reset.

And I say I'm okay for a while, until I remember why I'm not. Been lying to myself first most. I say my hope helps me cope. I'm just ignoring reality, trying to live in the stories I write once again. I'm not okay. When you asked me how I'm doing, I was lying. I'm not okay. Barely making it through the days. I'm really, just simply, not doing okay.

♬♪♫♪♫♪

Oh-hmm-oh-hmm. Don't want to get out of bed.
Oh-hmm-oh-hmm. Not sure what to write about anymore.
Oh-hmm-oh-hmm. I can smile, but I'm barely hanging on.
Oh-hmm-oh-hmm. What now? Where do I go from here?

Maybe I should turn to a higher power. Trust God to bring me peace. Follow after the countless people who've turned to their religion to help them make sense of the nonsense of life. But what do I do when my prayers just keep bringing me back to the reason I feel this way. I have all this built up inside of me, and I don't know what to do with it, so I think I've decided to give that over to God. That way I can keep going, knowing that my prayers may be answered in another place. That this song won't be lost to time, but if God really is out there listening he'll find ways and people who can sing it. And I'll never know, I'll just have to believe that love will find its way eventually.

So, I'm going to keep praying. I'll pray every day, and God will keep finding new ways. And maybe as the days turn to months I'll stop rewriting this song all the time. It won't cross my mind for weeks at a time, but the words will still be out there somewhere, and I hope that they're heard where they belong.

♬♪♫♪♫♪

Oh-hmm-oh-hmm. Don't want to get out of bed.
Oh-hmm-oh-hmm. Not sure what to write about anymore.
Oh-hmm-oh-hmm. I can smile, but I'm barely hanging on.
Oh-hmm-oh-hmm. What now? Where do I go from here?

How long have I been working on this song now? I return to it every few weeks just to add another set of rambling lines. Thinking that the next verse will be the one that makes it all make sense. Just one more coupling rhyme will make things okay. Just one more moment of time will make things alright. I've rewritten it time and time again. And I won't stop until I run out of words. Won't stop till I run out of time.

# Infatuation

Infatuated with a lady named melancholy.
Dancing in the dark with my despondency.
Falling through the trap door,
lying still on my apartment floor.

Biting fingernails, using the blood as blush.
Smearing mascara, eyes heavy with nothing.
Trying to clinically induce tears.
A deep embrace with my worst fears.
Twenty-three degrees, slip, ice on the road.
Singing by yourself, flat, out in the cold.
Pour a glass of distilled low spirits.
Down it like a whiskey of elegy lyrics.

Infatuated with a lady named melancholy.
Dancing in the dark with my despondency.
Falling through the trap door,
lying still on my apartment floor.

Infatuated with a lady named melancholy.
Dancing in the dark with my despondency.
Falling through the trap door,
lying still on my apartment floor.

# Lavender Dress

She sighed. I rolled my eyes.
Told me she was going to buy that dress one day.

I'll wear it to the park with my friends.
Share an entire bottle of wine.
I'll flirt with a girl till her cheeks turn red.
Makeout with her under the sunshine.

I watched as her world grew brighter.
The sadness she carried was pushed away for
thoughts of a world where she'd be happy.
Every tear would be worth it in the end.
I don't know how she does it.

She swayed like a flower in a field.
I stood firm like a potted rock.
Beautiful thoughts filled her mind.
I looked dead inside.

One day, she swore.
Held her hands to her chest.
A longing stare reflected in those eyes.
She let out a sniffle.
I could see the hope in her smile.
Told me she was going to buy that dress one day.

# Cry For Help

My friends are worried for me.
They want what's best for me,
have they considered that's not what I'm after.
Maybe I just hate myself and I hide it with laughter.
I promise you, "I'm okay,"
but I lie all the time.

Dropping hints disguised as jokes.
Disassociating any chance I get.
This is a cry for help. I need to get better.
This is a cry for help. I need to get better.
I need someone to listen to me. I need your help.
I might need a slap across the face,
because I want to get better.

I'm smart, I give good advice,
I just don't listen to said advice.
I enjoy the pain I get from not eating.
I love stories more than breathing.
I'm not stupid, I just act that way.
I'm not nervous, just miserable.

I've gotten comfortable with the familiarity
of self-obsessed tendencies.
I'm breaking myself down into fragments
so I can reverse engineer the broken pieces.
Say I'm at my happiest when I'm sad.
Pretending like that's okay.

Dropping hints disguised as jokes.
Disassociating any chance I get.
This is a cry for help. I need to get better.
This is a cry for help. I need to get better.
I need someone to listen to me. I need your help.
I might need a slap across the face,
because I want to get better.

I'll let you take advantage of my kindness
as long as you're willing to lie to me.
I'm okay with the abuse if I feel like I have a use.
You don't love me, that's fine, I don't either.
I didn't get here by looking out for myself.
I'd lean over a cliff to get a better look at you,
falling off the edge to be closer to you.
The fall may hurt,
but I claim I've gotten good at that part.

Do you see?
Someone that desperately needs a friend.
Tell them there's a better way to live.
Tell them you'll listen if they're willing to talk.
Tell them you're there, even on the hard days.
And maybe they'll finally understand
they're not all alone.

Dropping the disguise.
Disavowing my lies.
This is a cry for help. I hope you're listening.
This is a cry for help. I want to do better.
My friends, I promise you I will get better.

## chapter iii

# chronic back pain from sitting on a pew

can you hold two ideas in one hand?
two thoughts in one brain at the same time?
i won't let you inside my journal.
i have your respect and love, admiration and all.
but my sister, these letters don't tell the whole story.
but my brother, these are the politics of love.
hours of my life were spent right here,
lost in thought, lost in writing songs.
unsure if these words mean anything.

# Punching Bag

Standing to the side, sharp pains in mine.
Left my gloves on the floor, let my knuckles do the work.
Will keep going, even if they begin to bleed.
One punch after another,
my heavy breathing sounds like crying.

I used to love this,
but now you love me less.
Thought I was a fighter,
I'm just your punching bag.

Screaming inside, staying silent on the outside.
Blood dripping from every hit, tears from all your shit.
Thought I could handle this fight,
I thought I was ready for real life.
But the bruises under my eyes say otherwise.

I used to love this,
but now you love me less.
Thought I was a fighter,
I'm just your punching bag.

# Blasphemy & Rejection

God, I'm sorry.
I don't know what I did to deserve this hell.
Legs buckled in a chain café.
Jealous of the people I'm happy for,
angry at someone I care about.
Every word I speak is blasphemy,
lying for the sake of saving face.

God, forgive me.
I don't know what I did to deserve this hell.
I cursed the ground when I fell down.
Laughed when she said motherfucker.
Collapsing another hundred times in my mind.
My thousand yard stare when you're on your phone.
I pretend to not hear or see these things.
Disassociating from my body before my time.

God, save me.
I don't know what I did to deserve this hell.
Do you reject me for my politics or for who I am?
An unbearable prick, a self-obsessed hippie.
Attach all the blame to my name, it's all the same.
I confess my sins, maybe I'm not a good friend.
All my prayers for my sake, in love with every mistake.
So, dear God, carry this prayer away from me.
Bring some semblance of hope to my life, please.

# Inner Monologue

Can you hear me?
Can anyone hear me?
Hello?

What makes you any different than
all the other imaginary friends in my head?
I'm clearly struggling here.
Where have you been?
If these words meant something,
maybe I wouldn't be hurting inside.

Can you hear me? Can anyone hear me? Hello?

Crickets and whispers of the wind.
That's all you are. Another voice in my head.
My inner monologue come to life.
Centuries of stories about a promise.
Why did you leave me behind?

Can you hear me? Can anyone hear me? Hello?

I'm not mad. I'm just kinda lonely.
Been trying to act tough. I'm just a little kid.
Still scared and anxious.
Not entirely sure how to deal with these emotions.
I need you. I need you right now.
So, where have you been?

Can you hear me? Can anyone hear me? Hello?

Crickets and whispers of the wind.
That's all you are. Another voice in my head.

# Red Bench

Said I got seven things on my mind.
And that ain't no way to get to Heaven, right?
Oh Lord, I've been feeling a little blue.
So he told me, 'Young man, take it to the red bench.'

If only I could shut up and shut it out.
My pathological need to write.
As if what I say doesn't matter any other way.
But y'know, Jesus spoke in stories too.

With all the plans I need to make,
and conversations left to be had.
Some days the rain makes me sad,
so I'll wait till another sunny day.
And when we hold hands in that land,
won't we both have something beautiful.

And it's true I've been praying at church,
after 'Dear Lord,' all the words are about the angels.
I sat with them, fell from my grace with a sigh.

The man on the cross knows my heart.
I've been searching for some words to say.
But I'm done with this stupid book.
If I skipped ahead I bet the ending sucks.
I don't know, I haven't written that part yet.
I'm over the stories and spoken word,
the overanalysis of every emotion I've ever known.

Said I got seven things on my mind.
Save me from a hell of my own making.
Been seeing between what is black and white.
So I said, 'Jesus, I wrote another poem on the red bench.'

# Tonight Seems Like a Good Night to Start Drinking

And here we are.
Thought I knew better,
but you know best.
And I saw this coming.
I would stay silent,
my eyes frozen inside.
And you would feign concern.
My mind far from here,
distancing myself from the now.
And I try to hide only feet away.
Lost myself in my poetry,
learning the lesson I dreaded.
And they tell tales of marriage.
Someone crying to the side,
I refuse to make eye contact.
And that love felt foreign.
The expectations placed on us,
only twenty or so years old.
And it is all we all want.
To fall so deeply in love,
that the hurt stops hurting.
And we all said our goodnights.
With only one thing on my mind,
I need a drink.

# Courtyard

I sat in a courtyard this morning.
Heard wedding bells ringing.

I watched as people walked by.
Wondered where they were going.

I tapped my fingers against my knee.
Not entirely sure what was bothering me.

I sat in a courtyard this morning.
Heard laughter over the bushes.

I watched as people walked by.
Wondered if they were really happy.

I tapped my fingers against my knee.
Not entirely sure why I'm even here.

I sat in a courtyard this morning.
Heard the words repeated again.

I watched as people walked by.
Wondered why they believe the stories.

I tapped my fingers against me knee.
Not entirely sure who will ever understand me.

I sat in a courtyard this morning.
Heard wedding bells ringing.

# Panic Symptoms

All of a sudden I can't breathe.
My eyes keep falling out of focus.
I feel my face losing its color.
Manic, frantic, no words to say.
Headshake the words away.
Coughing for a breath,
a breath without feeling.
Falling from the ceiling.
Desperate for anything,
a thing that explains everything.
My throat closes up,
my eyes show me something else,
can't concentrate on anything else.
Dying as I'm trying to smile,
instead looking like I saw a ghost,
feeling most like a ghost myself.
Homesick close to home,
alone in my own family home.
My heart rapidly pumping blood,
draining itself of any love,
in love with what's drawing blood.
Experiencing the external symptoms
of my own internal panic, panicked
by my own love of feeling hypomanic.

# Am I Being Serious?

I can never tell if you're being serious.
What's imaginary and what's reality?
A little sarcastic and completely authentic.
Sums it up in a few words, what's true and what's you?
How do I know what's genuine and what's a ruse?

They don't believe a word I say.
Cried nonsense once too much.

Ask me over biscuits and coffee
what pages are embellished fairy stories
and which are letters to my friends.
Of the names on the paper, who is real,
and who is a reflection of my psyche?

They don't believe a word I say.
Cried nonsense once too much.

I can never tell if you're being serious.
Neither can I most of the time.
I'm always trying to tell a story.
Always trying to make something of myself.
Now I can't even tell the difference anymore.

*Joshua, is this poetry or is this lying?*

# Mayflower

History changes to fit the narrative.
Morality shifts to the needs of the rich.
The war songs they taught me as a kid
aren't the same ones being sung today.
Because this isn't the country I was raised in.

I'll bow my head towards the sky,
but as I walk the earth,
I won't serve a king a day I'm alive.

Woe to those.
Immigrants built this country.
They're not the ones killing it.
Woe to those.
I'm not the judge above, but let me say this,
the men you worship aren't Christians.
Woe to those who call evil good,
and good evil.

Stand in the synagogue. Stand in your church hall.
Beat your chest with a necklace made of wood.
Say a prayer to your God.
Get on your knees and beg for mercy.

No kings shall fly my flag.
My ancestors bled for the red.
My family paid for the blue.
We cried revolution once before.
We can do it again.

Samuel warned them. The nation fell apart.
The crowd cried crucify. The governor found no wrong.
Pilate asked, "Shall I crucify your king?"
They answered, "We have no king but Caesar."
And that's the story of how Jesus died.
Humans killed God so we could reign supreme.
It wasn't enough, we mock him with every idol we erect.
Build our towers towards the heavens.
Icarus flew where he shouldn't have.
God won't flood the earth. We will.
We'll keep raising the sea levels
till we burn in a hellfire of our own creation.

Stand on the senate floor. Stand in your town hall.
Carry the cross of the men who abuse you.
Say a prayer to your god.
Get on your knees and beg for a taste.

I'll say a prayer to my God. No kings a day I'm alive.
I'll say a prayer to my God. No kings a day I'm alive.
I'll say a prayer to my God. No kings a day I'm alive.
I'll say a prayer to my God.
Give me liberty or give me death.

I'll bow my head towards the sky,
but as I walk the earth,
I won't serve a king a day I'm alive.

# Christian Love

There's no hate like.
There's no place like this place.
There's no hate like.
There's no way you'll like what I have to say.

God can't hear you when you whisper on the side.
A gavel at the pulpit, a sword in my back pocket.
My heart on my sleeve, a black tattoo over my chest.
Only here can I hear a gunshot in four part harmony.

Follow the money, you won't have to follow far.
Preach love, teach kindness.
I saw the red hat you were wearing.
The words are only as strong as you let them be.

There's no hate like.
There's no place like this place.
There's no hate like.
There's no way you'll like what I have to say.

Belittle the little girls, make their hearts ashamed.
Behold the young boys, strike them in God's name.
For all that's holy separate our sister from her brother.
Act surprised when the two sides resent the other.

An accusation baked with love and smiles.
Tell them off, sleep on your almighty pedestal.
Point the finger, wash your hands upon this soapbox,
at least you didn't swear when you damned their soul.

Pray for your enemies. Pray for your family.
Pray for your friends. Pray for them all.
Bless their heart and God save their souls.

There's no hate like.
There's no place like this place.
I've heard it all.
The remarks made in the dark.
The lies we lift to the sky.
There's no hate like your love.
No love in the way you talk to me!

# Jesus Loves You (21st Century Version)

They got the song wrong.
What you sung in Sunday School
was just an early demo.

Jesus doesn't love you.
If you're poor or without a home.
Red, black, yellow, deport them all.
Jesus doesn't love you.
If you're trans or communist.
Palestinian, Iraqi, Ukrainian, bomb them all.

You had one vote.
Told me you love the Lord almighty.
Look at who you put in office.
Someone who said they believed in Jesus,
shot their neighbor on the way to Washington.

This is the American church.
Used the name in vain.
The Jesus they pray to ain't
the one who died for our sins.
Because that Jesus doesn't love you.

# Warriors and Angels

Raised them to serve the land.
To lift their voice hand in hand.
Tell the tales of warriors, in all their might.
Sing the songs of angels, wings shining bright.
Yet, do you hear the thunder in the ground?
I fear there's no harmony to be found.

Your children hate each other.
Lonely little creatures,
blaming the other for their sadness.

A warrior kneels on a hill all alone,
says he loves this girl back home,
but he treats her like an object to be won.
An angel cries to the skies,
says she wants a man to care for her,
but plays with him like a toy she can use.

Raised them to serve the land.
To lift their voice hand in hand.
Tell the tales of warriors, in all their might.
Sing the songs of angels, wings shining bright.

He blames her for his own wounds.
She faults him for her own sins.
And he was hurt by her words.
And she fears what he might do.
They hate each other.
Say they don't, hope to find love,
but they simply hate each other.

Tell the tales of warriors, in all their might.
Sing the songs of angels, wings shining bright.

# (Hard to) Hate Your Friend

I've read the verses, I know the rules,
but I also know my friend.
Jen, it's easier to hate a people you've never met.
We can deport the immigrants
before we get to know them.
We can throw stones at a gay couple
without saying a word.
But it's hard to hate your friend.

You and I have more in common than not.
We both pray every day. We both love music,
be it gospel hymns or another folk-rock band.
We both write like our lives depend on it.
You've taught me more about life by just being you
than I ever would've learned from watching the news.
We've each lost friends we still miss every day.
Neither of can go a moment without falling in love,
looking for the best in life, a person to love who we are.
And it would seem we have similar taste in women.

The world is a scary place.
We fear what we don't know.
But it's hard to hate your friend.
Been told to not trust a stranger.
We mock what we don't know.
But it's hard to hate your friend.

You and I have more in common than not.
We both smile at all the same small things,
be it a drink with a friend,
autumn night, or laughing baby.
We both take walks just to feel like ourselves.
I punch people for a living,
you punch people to keep living.
You're an outspoken socialist,
and I'm still trying to hold plausible deniability.
Neither of us can go a minute without dreaming,
there I am dancing, feeling the music, just like you.
And I know we both just want to be seen as pretty.

The world is a scary place.
We fear what we don't know.
But it's hard to hate your friend.
Been told to not trust a stranger.
We mock what we don't know.
But it's hard to hate your friend.

Hard to hate someone you love.

# Morning Prayer

Hey God, I hope you're having a good morning.
Are you as troubled by the world as I am?
There's war, another just started.
Every morning is another soul's goodnight.
Do you ever think it would be better if
you just didn't get out of bed this morning?
Obviously not, you're omnipresent and all that,
but I have to imagine you still know the pain
of watching the sun rise over a country on fire.

Or do you still see the good in us?
The little things that make us human.
Two people falling in love.
A beautiful winter morning in my hometown.
A group of friends staying by one another's side.
Kind words shared like poetry.
Here we are on the precipice of a new day,
do you also wonder about the wonder of it all?

Personally, I'm having a good morning.
Another day where I'm happy to be alive.
I often let the world's worries rest on me,
it's a lot, I don't know how you handle it.
But this morning, all I can see is the little things.
The things that make life beautiful.
God, I hope you're having a good morning.

# Purpose

I saw a ghost today. A soul wandering the mainland.
An echoing call helplessly rung.
A common theme these days.
I saw a ghost yesterday.
And the day before that, and every day.

People my age are depressed.
The chemicals messed up our brains.
Aimless. An entire generation with no where to go.
Beyond that, there's nothing beyond here.
No purpose to their lives.

I saw a ghost today. A soulless stare met my eyes.
The moans fill the room silently,
crying out for a reason, any reason.
I wish the answer to life was a simply given one,
but I can't ask a question that doesn't belong to me.

There are old folks and young ones who are lost.
They don't know their purpose here.
Living with unfinished business while
they still have time to finish it.
They're hurting. And I can't help but hurt for them.

You're not going to find reason in the season.
No amount of money, no accomplishments, no person.
I can't give your life meaning.
You have to look inside, find a purpose in life.
Give yourself a reason.
A reason to get out of bed in the morning.
A reason to be a good person.
A reason to smile when you're sad.
There is no answer found on day one.
Life is for finding meaning, everchanging as it may be.
Some find it in connection. Some find it in religion.
Some find it in art. I've found a little in each part.

I saw a ghost today.

# Praying at 10:58am on a Sunday

Hey, it's me. I'm trying to focus, but I just had a frozen coffee and now my heartbeat has other plans. They're about to pass around the communion trays. I'm trying to remember something, something that I already know, but often the things I know are the things I take for granted.

One of my favorite Bible verses actually comes from that night. Y'know, the one where Jesus and his friends ate their last dinner together. "Love one another as I love you. Greater love has no one than this, that someone lay down his life for his friends." And Jesus died for his friends less than twenty-four hours later. I want to be a good friend. That's what this whole book is about. Been working on it all year, that part hasn't changed at least. But God, I'm afraid I've come up short. I can't even lay down my own doubt and insecurities, let alone life. I hope my family and friends know I wasn't trying to let them down.

The world is falling apart; I don't want to be the one to say crucify. Everything seems so political, but was Jesus not killed for the same reasons? Not much has really changed. And I talk, but what am I going to do about it? Soj was right, I've been a mess lately. Can't even sit through this church service without having another panic attack. Barely can stomach this tiny little wafer without my body shutting down. I'm not even capable of eating like a normal person, why do all these people think I can actually make a difference? Do they not see the same sad, little, punk child I see? They believe in me, wish I could say the same.

I'll proudly proclaim I believe in you, or so I say in my head. I wonder what the feeling was that night when the bread was handed out and Judas left the room. I say I'm your friend, but how quickly would I betray everyone I know? Maybe I wouldn't, but what about Peter? I wish I could say I would never deny you, though I know that's not true. So, I want to say sorry. Please forgive me. I'm young, I'm afraid I'll deny you more than just three times. I want to be better. I apologize for all those times I fail you. God, that's the easy part to say. I need to apologize for all the times I'm going to fail myself. I vow to make all these apologies come true.

Here I am. Breaking bread, drinking juice. Wish I could concentrate on this for more than two seconds. My mind keeps going back to this book. So far all these pages have been built on my tears and worst fears. Jesus, can I ask you a question? What did the sky look like in Gethsemane? How did you deal with the feeling of being alone? Your friends nowhere to be seen. What stopped you from running away?

If this life really means something, if you really died just to free me, then maybe it's time for me to make the most of it. No more writing with my eyes closed. I'll fight back against my demons. I'll finish this prayer with a smile. And this book, it will become a love letter to everyone who calls me their friend. I'll love each of them as you loved me.

chapter iv

# two ghosts sharing human stories around a campfire

we first met at the cabin, out by the firepit.
she looked like a cross of a hippie and preacher.
nice to meet you, i told her, my name's soj.
he spoke dryly, yet he was calm and welcoming.
told him i like to go by the name jenna.
she asked me if life here gets better.
he told me there's no reason to be scared.
the monsters and ghouls won't hurt you here.
the pain of the world won't stay with us dear.
jenna, stay by the fire with me, i'll protect you.
soj, you can smile now, i can care for both of us.

# The Cabin

I've known Joshua since he was, let's see,
I wanna say sixteen. Maybe it was seventeen.
We used to argue all the time.
I would get sick of his immaturity.
To be fair to him, I was a bit of a jerk.
One time we got in a fight
and he punched me in the nose.
Ha, that skinny little kid bloodied my entire face.
But that's behind us now.
These days I like to think we're closer than ever.
Anyway, let me show you around.

Welcome to the cabin.
A place to go when the rest of the world is just too much.
Back in high school
Joshua would come here all the time.
We would chat. He would daydream.
He once told me this was the one place
where his anxiety didn't feel crushing.

The room arrangement is a bit awkward, sorry.
It was Joshua's way of sorting his thoughts.
He tried so many things to keep his brain on track.
Color coding, to-do lists,
there was a place for everything.
And when everything was too overwhelming
he could just close the door to that particular room.
I don't think it ever really helped.
But I do know it gave him a moment to breathe.

Here's the backyard. We used to come out here
and toss a football around every day.
A breath of fresh air never hurt anyone.
He and I running up the score,
nothing could stop us.
He would ride his green razor scooter
as far as those old wheels would take him.
Dreaming up new stories, retelling old ones.
Stories of superheroes, pro fighters,
and Oklahoma's greatest mysteries.
He would cast his friends in the starring roles.
Other times he would create some new character:
that's how you and I got here, right?

He always did have quite the imagination.
Unfortunately, it would sometimes run rampant.
You see that forest out there?
The trees are pretty from afar
but be careful if you go near,
there's monsters lurking in those woods.
They're the remains of an unchecked imagination,
an anxious ideal turned into acres of unbridled fear.
Left alone, the fear only grows.

Alright, well there's the house tour.
It's pretty quiet around here these days.
Joshua isn't around as much anymore.
He's out there, living his life. Good for him.
I'll be honest though–promise not to tell him this–
I miss the time we used to waste in here.
Writing comic books. Playing football.
But hey, this is his story after all.
I just feel like there's so much left in this old place,
voices that are just waiting to be heard.
Imagine that.

# Hey God, You There?

Hey God, you there?
It's Jen. There's a lot going on,
so if you have the time,
I would love to tell you what's on my mind.

Do you see me walking down the street,
wondering how I wound up here?
Am I wandering or am I just feeling wary?
I want to be pretty. I said I could figure it out,
a life of femininity and sexuality,
but when faced with the factuality,
I realized you can't love what's not there.

I might leave. It's nothing personal,
I just need a change of scenery.
I still believe in you. At least I think I do.
I still love you; you'll still love me, won't you?
When I came out of those waters
they called me a new person in your eyes.
Can I do it again?
I'll die to my past if it writes my name anew.

I'm not the girl you want me to be.
Not the daughter my father raised.
But I'm me. And there's nothing I'd rather be.
I hope people smile when they see mine again.
I've lived too long without one.

Thank you for this gorgeous evening.
A day that makes me feel likewise.
I love you. And I hope it makes you happy
to see me finally learning to love myself.

# Not a Poet

I'm not the poet in the story.
I write the email that gets you in the door.
Tracking the numbers in a spreadsheet,
writing the code that will show your words.

Analytical, they call me.
The one who makes sure the chores are taken care of
so you can write your little stories.
I'm your conscience, not your emotions.
I know my job isn't glorious, it wasn't meant to be.
You're the artist, she's the pretty one,
I'm just the one who gets shit done.

I don't mean to complain,
I can clock in for the 9 to 5,
but you're back in charge for the fun times,
only inviting me when you need someone
to pick you up off the floor.
That's all I'm here for.

I'll protect you from your worst fears.
Tell you what you already know,
say it in a way that you can understand.
I give you permission to be yourself,
standing guard while you cry and laugh.

I'm whoever you need me to be.
Your best friend, your coach, your protector,
but I'm not a poet.

# Silvia and Jenna

*Silvia*

Sweetie, what are you running from?
You don't need to wear a jacket in the summer.
You won't be more of yourself if you hide away.
I've always known you were beautiful.

*Jenna*

Where do I go from here?
Do these cuts on my face really make me pretty?
Can the makeup make up for the fact I am who I am?
I'm a nobody. An imaginary girl. A forgotten dream.

*Silvia*

I think you're more like me than you know.
And I know you don't really know who that is.
I've held the pain in the palm of my hands,
but I learned to love where I could overcome.

*Jenna*

Every morning I dread stepping out into the world.
I hear the birds singing; I wish I lived like them.
Every evening I'm afraid to be seen.
I hear the people laughing; I want to be one of them.

*Silvia*

I didn't move on because it was easy.
Every day I told myself I want to get better,
until one day I had. Learned it was okay to let go of
my past, it was the only way to become who I am now.

*Jenna*

I see her, I feel her, where did she go?
The girl I fell in love with, the one I said I would be.
I see her, I feel her, why do I hide her away?
Oh God, let me let go. Let me love that girl again.

# The Third Voice

You could never tell this story without me.
You pretend like I'm not real.
I promise you, my friend,
I'm only as imaginary as you let me be.
So, don't blame me. You chose to step in that ring.
It's not my fault you couldn't roll with the punches.

I'm the third voice in your head.
The one you say you hate
but talk with on the daily.
You pray to God to take me away
then invite me in the front door.

*Soj, my friend, why do you put up with this idiot?*
*You're too smart to deal with his indecisive bullshit.*
*Maybe I'd finally respect you again if you*
*just spoke your mind and told him to get a life.*
*Jenna, doll, you aren't fooling anyone.*
*You naïve little girl, he doesn't really love you.*
*The world doesn't see you like you want them to,*
*all they see is a troubled silhouette.*

I'm the third voice in your head.
The one who is honest with you,
tells you what the other two won't.
You pray to God to give you peace,
but my friend, peace is earned.

# Baseball Cap

People will often ask me,
"Hey Soj, why do you always wear a baseball cap?"
And I tell them to mind their own 'effin business.
Joshua told me I'm not allowed to swear as much anymore.
I'd call him a twit if it wasn't my job to look out for him.

Got approximately eight caps hanging in my room.
Enough for each day of the week, plus some.
Wear one when I don't want to brush my hair,
which to be fair, is pretty much always.

I would watch TV, watch a football game,
not have to worry about all the things bothering me.
When the world felt like it was closing in,
I could always get a breath of fresh air
by going out back to practice my free throw.

During the years when my anxiety controlled me,
talking sports was an easy way to be friendly.
Useless stats, meaningless facts, things seemed okay.
I made friends while tossing a ball back and forth.
I had something in common with people,
felt like I was a part of a team.

Back when I hated the way I saw myself,
a baseball cap was something to hide under.
Now those hats sit on my shelf,
next to a photo frame, next to a jewelry box,
and when I wear one I never fail to feel like I belong.

# Apple

Do you like your name?
Does the past bring you shame?

Let's go to the orchard together.
Pick apples, place them in our baskets,
looking for the one that will catch our eye.

Drizzle it in caramel or bake a pie,
slice it up or eat it whole.
I used to eat red apples,
this time I'm looking for a green one.

Let's go to the orchard together.
Pick apples, place them in our baskets,
looking for the one that will catch our eye.

The perfect one may fall,
as bittersweet as change ever is.
When it touches my tongue,
I'll recognize the taste right away.

# Oklahoma Girl

She grew up in a town on the plains,
listening to the wind hum as it rains.
Oh my, my Oklahoma Girl.
Born and raised under the blue skies.
She and her girl go to church every Sunday.
Lunch with her parents on their back porch.
Got red dirt stains on her denim jeans.
Oh my, my Oklahoma Girl.

The wind blows hair all over her face,
but beneath she's got a smile that'll put you to ease.
She's well-mannered, with a yes ma'am and a please,
always there to hold the door open for her lady,
was taught to say thank you and you're welcome.
Said she looks up to her mama,
wants to be as strong as her one day.
She'll make her proud of the girl she raised.

On the choir but couldn't hold a tune, bless her heart.
But I'll tell you, that girl can turn a prayer to a hymn.
Got all the beauty of a rose, rocking out in the back of bars.
Fell in love with a kid who grew up in Guthrie.
Got family living from Catoosa to Comanche,
and she'll never forget her home back in Moore.
Those hellscape traffic lights will never change.
Just wait, I'm sure a twister will take 'em out one day.

She grew up in a town on the plains,
listening to the wind hum as it rains.
Oh my, my Oklahoma Girl.
Born and raised under the blue skies.
She and her girl go to church every Sunday.
Lunch with her parents on their back porch.
Got red dirt stains on her denim jeans.
Oh my, my Oklahoma Girl.

She lives west of the railroad tracks.
Travels up to the city at least once a month.
Every Saturday in the fall watches college ball.
Could tell you the name of every starter on her Sooners.
Find her out back, balancing a beer in her left hand
while throwing a tight spiral with her right.
To hell with Texas,
they got nothing on the state she loves.

Will get into a fight with the best of them,
then buy you a coffee as long as you shake her hand.
Says this is a place where people are kind and hospitable,
ain't no conman who will change that.
See her knockin' on doors all morning long,
won't rest if there's good to be done.
But just know, she'll never miss a chance to talk crap
about those bums over on Lincoln Boulevard.

*Jenna, baby, you know you ain't ever leaving.*
*There may be better places to call your home,*
*but there's only one Oklahoma.*

She grew up in a town on the plains,
listening to the wind hum as it rains.
Oh my, my Oklahoma Girl.
Oh my, my Oklahoma Girl.
I'll remember those sunsets as long as I live.
There's no place like that place,
cause where else would I find you?
Oh my, my Oklahoma Girl.

# Does Family Last Forever?

*hey, it's me, your daughter, your sister, your niece, your granddaughter. i wrote you this song, i hope you listen to it. i love you. and always will.*

*- signed, jenna*

Does family last forever? *and ever*
Is there a limit to your love?
You told me there wasn't.
I'm not sure that's true.
Is blood thicker than whatever else?
Does family stick together? *now and never*
I hope the answer is yes.
But I'm not so sure.

Can you still look at me without being disappointed?
Y'know, if so, maybe you'd look and see
just how happy I am.
I don't know if you'll understand,
I don't know if I need you to,
I just know I need you still.

Are you ashamed of me?
I thought family stuck up for one another.
I would take a punch for you, but you can't even
protect my name from ridicule and misuse!
Your friends sneer at you on my behalf,
do you blame them or blame me?
Maybe I'm too much of a liability for you.
Maybe I'm not worth it to you anymore.
And there's no maybe about why.

Does family last forever? *and ever*
Is there a limit to your love?
You told me there wasn't.
I'm not sure that's true.
Is blood thicker than whatever else?
Does family stick together? *now and never*
I hope the answer is yes.
But I'm not so sure.

All I'm asking for is a little respect,
the kind we all deserve.
Have I not done enough to earn that?
Does my appearance matter more than my character?
That's not what you said when I was growing up.
You all told me to look on the inside,
but for whatever reason it's different now.

I don't regret the memories we built.
I'm never going to burn the photos.
Every birthday, growing older together.
The holidays, the games, the meals, my family.
I can hear you telling me I'll always be your little kid,
but it's the way you say it that tells me you don't get it.
You say you'll love me no matter what,
do you not see the irony in that?
Please understand I'm not going away,
but I can't stay someone I'm not.
If you love me, let me love myself too.

Does family last forever? *and ever*
Is there a limit to your love?
You told me there wasn't.
I'm not sure that's true.
Is blood thicker than whatever else?
Does family stick together? *now and never*
I hope the answer is yes.
But I'm not so sure.

# Foggy Nights

*Cloudy Eye's Lament*

I'm the one you see on all your foggy nights.
One step, two step, evade, you won't escape.
Friend, you walk the path of a sinner.
I'm no devil, no guardian angel, you know who I am.
Front kick, follow with a jab, carry your cross,
pinned with the weight of who you are.

There's no one else in this ring with us.
Just you, me, and the things you need to hear.
Stop sparring with your self-pity,
and start fighting with assertion.
Anxiety is just a fool's excuse,
you and your little feelings are a distraction.
You want to get better, right?
Then shut up and fight.

I'm your greatest friend.
The only one who isn't pretend.
I won't sugarcoat reality from you.
I don't treat you like a little kid.
You're not a damsel in distress.

If you can't handle reality just go run and cry to
your little imaginary boyfriend and girlfriend.
You really think you can trust them?
You know they're lying to you, right?
They say they have your best interest at heart,
but won't even be honest with you.
I'm the only one you can trust.
I'm the one who tells it like it is.
I won't be nice about this, I don't care what you think,
I'm here to remind you who you really are.

I'm the one you see on all your foggy nights.
One step, two step, evade, you won't escape.
Friend, you walk the path of a sinner.
I'm no devil, no guardian angel, you know who I am.
Front kick, follow with a jab, carry your cross,
pinned with the weight of who you are.

Iron sharpens iron, my friend.
Your poetry is better because of me.
You said it yourself, art hits best in the dark.
Blood and sweat can build so much more.
So, wipe your tears, conquer your fears,
and let's go another round trading blows.
You want to get better, right?
Then shut up and fight.

Forget your mom, she's too blinded by love.
Forget your sister, forget Isabella,
they don't know you like I do.
Forget James, forget your dear Mr. Auhsoj,
they could never be as good a friend as me.

I'm the one you see on all your foggy nights.
One step, two step, evade, you won't escape.
Friend, you walk the path of a sinner.
I'm no devil, no guardian angel, you know who I am.
Front kick, follow with a jab, carry your cross,
pinned with the weight of who you are.

I'm the one you see on all your foggy nights.
You want to get better, right?
Then shut up and fight.

# Pretty Girls

Got a little dressed up tonight.
Shaved legs, makeup on my face, a new pair of heels.
Sitting at the bar, feeling hot as heck.
Talk with a few strangers, the game on the TV.
Bottom of the eighth, Mariners up by 2 runs.
And that's when she walks in with her friends.
I try not to stare, but damn girl, you're so pretty.
She sits down next to me and orders a drink.
Vodka tonic, drop the lime in.

Why do girls have to be so pretty?
It's honestly too distracting.
Can't concentrate on anything besides her.
Her face, her laugh. Her grace, her ass.
It's all so enchanting.
Don't like to assume, but you look like the kinda gal
who may just have a little chemistry with me.
And you're definitely my type: A hot girl.

We could kiss, I could be your miss.
Oh, here comes another shot I'll miss.
Don't know what to say, don't want to mess this up.
Thinking to myself, "Jenny, just tell her she's pretty."
A compliment never hurt anyone.
But she's the kind who can
break your heart into a million pieces.

When we get to chatting I can feel my heart beating.
You're such a flirt, I'm such a mess, but I digress.
I want to take you home, take off your clothes,
but the voice in my head says otherwise.
Was told to be ashamed of this body.
Could I live with the guilt of my sin?
Would do anything to hear that laugh all night,
but I'll lie to avoid lying in your sheets.
God would be proud of me, right?
I'm not sure why he would, I'm just a coward.

Don't mind me, some twenty-something.
Praying on my doorsteps every morning.
Thinking about sex and wine in the evening.
Trying to make sense of it all.

We could kiss, I could be your miss.
Oh, here comes another shot I'll miss.

# Invisible

You named me after a comic book character.
The superhero you created for yourself.
An inverted version of who you want to be.
But Joshua, I'm no superhero, no paragon.
I can't save you, all I can be is your friend.
Hopefully I'm a good one.

When asked if you could choose one superpower
you picked to be invisible.
Built a whole secret identity around
not being able to be seen.
In the comics you were seen as the team leader,
and the irony of that isn't lost on me.

All these characters you turn to for advice.
Do you know where the alter ego ends and you begin?
I'm the rationalization of your inner thoughts,
the common sense to your worry and doubt.

Hey dude, please listen to me.
That's all I'm here for.
You shouldn't try to disappear in the daylight.
You can't live in the frame of a comic book.
Don't create conflict just for the sake of the plot.
I'm the invisible one, the friend in your head,
let me thwart those supervillains for you instead.
But you have to, and I mean this,
you have to be the one to go out into the world.
Don't hide your face, don't make yourself invisible.
Stand up and fight, lead with confidence.
Be a paragon for what's right.
Be who you really are.

# Some Advice

I sit down on the empty barstool next to you.
With a smile, pull the mask off my face.
Flash a ten and order a White Russian.
You try to ignore me, but I know you just want to talk.
So, I ask you how you've been.
"Was doing good until you arrived."

I've got some advice for you, boy.
You have an over-reliance on your lead leg.
The way you switch your guard before you kick is a tell.
All I have to do is jam you at the knee
and counter with an uppercut to the jaw.

"Why are you here? What do you want?"
I want to help you. You think I like seeing you lose?
Not at all. I fear you've become too content with such things.
The man I know is better than that.
He doesn't waste his time by crying.
He sucks it up. Acts tough. He keeps punching.

I've got some advice for you, boy.
You put an over-emphasis on your emotions.
I'm not friends with cowards, so man up.
Don't listen to those puny voices in your head,
you're not depressed, you're just fine.
You just need to stop being such a pansy.

"You really think so? I mean, Soj keeps telling me-"
Don't you dare listen to that imbecile.
He's a loser hippie. He's not a fighter like us.
We're winners, you understand?
We don't throw the towel in, we just punch harder.

# I'll Be Okay

I don't mean to sour the mood. This isn't meant to hurt you. I never intended to cause any pain.

I'll be okay. We don't have to say goodbye forever, I just need a little space. Room to grow. Figure out who I am. I'm going to go and fall in love with everything I can.

For so long I tried to mask my imperfections
as I built up a mountain of internal stress.
I've lived my life on a foundation of fear;
scared of heights, guns, dying, and hell.
Most of all I was scared of myself.
Thought life was an exam I had to ace.
But I'm starting to realize to believe,
you first have to believe in yourself.

I'm not here to pretend I'm an angel
when I know we all have our demons.
Don't tell me I've changed
when I've always been this way.
It's not my fault that you never looked close enough.
No one tricked me, I wasn't lied to,
this is just the person I am.
And I like to think I'm pretty good person:
I have dreams, I have fears, I love life,
how does that make me any different?

I'll be okay. I promise you. This isn't anyone's fault. Life is about more than good and evil. Please don't worry about me. I'll be okay. I don't regret anything. I'm not forsaking who I've been. Life was always meant to be something great.

Have you ever had a deep feeling something's wrong?
You can only pretend it's not for so long.
I tried, I really did, but that's not me.
I would be lying to everyone if I said otherwise.
You can't say you're a good person
if you believe everything you see is bad.
I tried, I really did, but you can only
pretend you're not yourself for so long.

You can pray for me,
but please don't try to change me.
You can say I'm a bad person, but you should know,
I've been calmer lately. I'm nicer, less self-obsessed.
More caring than I once was.
Maybe it's okay to have a little doubt in life.
Maybe we're not supposed to know everything.
There's more than one way through the forest.
I'm going to stop drowning under the water,
finally come out into the world.
I don't need to hold myself down to fly.

I'll be okay. I promise you. This isn't anyone's fault. Life is about more than good and evil. Please don't worry about me. I'll be okay. I don't regret anything. I'm not forsaking who I've been. Life was always meant to be something great.

This song goes out to anyone who has ever loved me. Trust me, I'll be okay. And in case you're wondering, I am happy. I really am. Hopefully you feel the same way. No matter where I go in life, I'll always remember you. And I'll always love you.

# Lost Dog

"Where you going, Soj?" she asked.
Just going on a short walk.
"Alright, be safe," she said returning to her book.
Zipped my hoodie, locked the door behind me.

No music this time. I keep my eyes sharp.
The dog got out of his cage again.
A bark just as bad as the flesh in his teeth.
I'd put the beast to sleep if I could.

The audacity he has to call himself man's best friend.
Hate foams from his mouth, forms a puddle of drool.
He's nothing more than a monster,
controlled by his master, his own fear and resentment.

I find him sitting alone at the train station,
treating his calloused knuckle wounds.
He whistles at me, "Come here, boy!"
Not an ounce of empathy left in his voice.

Cloudy Eye, I know you don't like me.
The feeling is mutual, I can assure that much.
For all the harm you've done,
you can die in hell all alone.

I know you've been talking to them behind my back.
You can insult me till the moon grows old,
but if you lay even a finger on that girl
I'll show you what real fear looks like.
She deserves to not live in constant fear
of someone like you.
Don't diminish her beauty,
don't demonize her existence.

I don't understand why he still keeps you around.
The pain you cause all of us.
You drag him around like a chew toy,
try to bury him like an old bone.
Mark my word sir, one day he will kill you.
I know you think he isn't strong enough,
and maybe he isn't yet, but he will be.
Love will always be stronger than hate.
You won't break him, I won't let you.
I'll protect him, coach him to beat you.

He wraps his hand around my throat.
"Stay away from me, Soj," he says.
I spit in his eye. He doesn't seem to care.
"Our job is to keep him safe,
you're just mad I'm better at it."
His breath reeks from all the lies.
"I'm not the one who's lost his way,
the one pushing his every emotion away.
Soj, you're nothing more than a fool."

# The Girl in the Poem

Are you going to blame the president?
It's always the Republicans' fault, never yours.
Excuses don't change who we are.
There's a reason you and I don't see eye to eye.
I just need you to admit it, please.
I'm strong enough, I can handle the truth,
let's not just choose to ignore this.

I bet you were talking with that girl again.
She's beautiful. Go, tell her how you feel.
You flirt like a conservative,
and get your heart broken like a lost man.
But as long as you're happy, I will be.

You have your poetry, I have a lifeline.
A bottle of tequila and a stuffed bra.
You have your friends, I have a sweater.
Razor burn and new perfume.

Haven't worn any makeup since Halloween.
Has the sadness from that night still not subside?
I'm the girl walking down
a boulevard of her broken dreams.
We lost, alright. And now I have to lose you too.
Accidently cut myself on the edge of hope.
Estrogen won't help me bleed any more.

And you'll say I made you a better man.
It was never my plan to be your stepping stone.
But I love you. I hope you do to.
Let's not ignore this any longer.

# Unfinished

Will you ever finish your first book?
Ever write past the first few chapters?
What a grand tale you had in mind,
time travel, vikings, sci-fi, secret spies.
For all that, you said it was the people
in the story that fascinated you.
You told me each character was based
off a different part of your personality.
So, what ever happened to them?

I'm afraid you'll leave my story unfinished too.
Only keep me around as long as I'm relevant to you.
I know I'm just a side character,
you're the protagonist.
But I have so much more about me left to learn.
Remember our high school days,
they disappeared before I got to say goodbye.
You never realize the parts of you that died
while you were focused on just staying alive.
What ever happens to me when you outgrow
the need for what my voice represents?

Your friend till the end.
An ending that will never be written,
for I fear my story will be left unfinished.

# That Kid

Would little me be proud of me?
Would that kid think I'm pretty?
I've made mistakes. I've changed a lot.
Do you still see the love in my eyes?

See me, smiling again, remember that feeling?
And my skin is glowing in the sun,
dressing freely, dressing like me.
To hell with their rules.
Hey me, life is kinda crazy sometimes.
You're going to have bad days. But you'll be okay.
You're going to have some of the best days ever,
in those moments don't let your anxiety tell you otherwise.

What would you say if you saw me dancing at the bar?
Heard me cussing in the kitchen while making dinner.
If you saw me kiss a girl would you try to pray for my soul?
Walk in the door, my clothes on her bedroom floor.

At what point did my family start to see
someone different? Was it gradual or crushing?
On what day did God forsake me?
Or was that just my own self-hate speaking?
I promised them I would stay faithful,
they say the drugs changed me.
Dear, was it not for the better?
It didn't make me weak, not all change kills you,
I'm stronger than I've ever been.

There will be a day when you don't believe in prayer.
There will be times when you hate who you are.
There will be years where you feel distant
from who you were.
Trust me, the hard times won't last forever.
You will have your heart broken.
You will question everything about yourself.
You will regret the rash decisions you've made.
Growing up will be scary.
But you're so smart, I know you can figure it out.
Kid, I figure that's just part of life.

Listen to me, you can listen to yourself.
The outside noise will get distracting,
so learn to take the time to hear your heart beating.
Life's complicated, you'll realize that before nine.
It doesn't ever really make more sense,
the beauty of sex and religion will make you cry,
simple things like eating will become challenging,
and you'll find honesty hurts more than any lie.

If I could just go back in time,
see you playing in that frontyard again,
look you in those brownish green eyes,
tell you I love you and I'm so sorry,
sorry for the heartache I'll cause you.
I'm so proud of you, kid.
I hope you're not disappointed to see who we become.

Would little me be proud of me?
Would that kid think I'm pretty?
Am I the woman you thought you'd see?

# RE: Internalized Hate and Beauty Standards

I hope this reaches you well.
What the hell, let's cut the formalities.
I've got something to say
and I ain't playing any games.

I need you to hear me, my dear,
you must stop hanging around that man.
He's nothing but evil.
Wants nothing but you dead.
If he isn't the one to do it,
he will hand the knife over to you
and let you do it for yourself.

You chase his approval.
He holds it above your head like a prize.
Every time he says you're pretty
it feels like you're winning.
He makes you earn it,
only will say those words if you hide
every little part of you that he hates.

Stop entertaining the slurs.
Don't invite his hate into your life.
There's enough of that already,
you don't need it from yourself too.

A little more blush,
he says it'll never be enough.
Tear the hair from your skin,
more pain is no way for change.

Jenna, my love,
you're a gorgeous woman.
Never forget that.

# I'll Hold You Now

Soj, I see you.
You are appreciated.
I know how tough this is; life ain't always easy.
You're allowed to cry too.
Rest your head on my shoulder, dude.
I'll listen to it all,
every last thing you've held inside.

It can be exhausting to live every day,
but there's no one better at it than you.
You're there for the good and bad,
and stay positive when it's all just numb.
I hope you see the importance of that.
You're so patient with us.
I've seen the way you bring him back to earth.
You call me a flower when I feel like dirt.
And no one is better at seeing past all the mist.

Mr. Strong Man, Mr. I've Got This,
you won't let us down when you're feeling down.
You need us just as much as we need you.

Soj, I see you.
You are valid. You are loved.
No one is immune to the heaviness of life.
You're allowed to cry too.
Rest your head on my shoulder, dude.
I'll listen to it all,
every last thing you've held inside.

chapter v

# broken hearts are the leading cause of broken ukulele strings

if only,

the lipstick didn't run dry.

if only,

i knew how to write a better song.

if only,

identity and love weren't so intrinsically tied.

if only,

my heart was calloused to feeling pain.

if only,

i could understand why i don't eat well.

if only,

i could look myself in the eyes with a smile.

# Standing in a Rainstorm

I wish I didn't have to feel sad to write my best poetry.
Half the time I write, I like to imagine
I'm standing in the middle of a rainstorm,
reciting these words to the reflection in a puddle.
My voice cracks, my tears disguised by rain.
I look up towards Heaven's sky and cry out,
hoping for the ground to shake, the wind to howl,
anything that will let me know I'm not alone here.
Looking for anyone who will listen to me.
I'd even give this poem to the squirrel in a tree
if he'd hug me after. Anything to be seen.

But truth be told,
I wrote this in a coffee shop
while drinking a caramel latte.
I'm not as messy as I want you to think I am.
I don't write in my journal that much,
this poem was written on an excel spreadsheet.
And I know I'm an emotional mess,
because that's what I put on my business card.
My creativity has a personal stake in my mental state,
so I play it up, let myself be all depressed,
because I know my words are more interesting that way.
And I don't know if I like what that says about me.

I wish I didn't have to feel sad to write my best poetry.
I wish I didn't have to stand in a rainstorm
to think the way I feel matters at all.

# The Lie We All Tell Ourselves

I'm talking like things will change.
Not right now, sure, but in the future.
And they won't. I know better than that.
But I just need something to keep me smiling
until I'm back on my feet again.

Things would change if I was just a better writer.
My next letter or song will show you all.
Give it two years, let's say.
I'll have grown, things will be different,
that's when it will all make sense.
It all sounds so nice.
The pain will have been worth it in the end.

Ifs and maybe thens I tell my friends.
They nod along, but their eyes sing another song.
I see that they can see what I've yet to perceive.
Please tell me there's hope,
because I'm not ready to accept there's not.

Telling stories in my head.
Calculating odds that should equal zero.
I'm lying to myself, and I know it.
Just won't admit it. Please, I need this.
You and I. A world not at war. My big break.
I'm happy. Doesn't that all sound nice?
I don't care that it's all a lie.
I just need a reason to keep smiling.

# Make Believe

Let's play a game of pretend.
You'll pretend to like me,
and I'll pretend to be emotionally stable.

Sorry to break it to you,
but our friendship ain't a real one.
I've seen this one before, you'll leave me eventually.
Why bother getting invested when it's inevitable.
I know you're just humoring me
because I've never said anything that funny.
Let's cut to the chase, I'm a loser,
everyone learns that in time.

I've created new friends in my head
and been acting like that's normal.
I think it helps me compartmentalize.
He has his life so much more together than me.
She is more in touch with her emotions than I ever could be.
I've got them, I don't need anyone else.
They would all think I'm crazy anyway.
And y'know, they might have a point.

Let's play a game of pretend.
You'll pretend to like me,
and I'll pretend that isn't just reality.

You told me in your own way you like being around me.
Probably when you showed up randomly at my house
or when you answered my text in little time.
I still said to myself, they're just acting nice,
be careful, you wouldn't want to hurt yourself.
And when I heard myself say that aloud
I started to wonder if I was my own abusive friend.
Too mesmerized by the past to see I'm playing pretend.

# Violently Shaking

When I go into my mind I like to find
the biggest, meanest lookin' guy around
and challenge him to a fight.
He's a couple drinks in, I'm stone-cold sober.
That's usually when I make my worst decisions.

I can always get a few good punches in
before I remember who I am.
Bloodied hands, broken speech, dizzy eyes.
I stumble around the room,
telling everyone I can keep fighting.

Soj pulls me aside, asks me why I do this to myself.
I tell him I'm fine. Not the first time he's heard that lie.
I'm violently shaking. My eyes keep falling out of focus.
He asks me what I've ate today. I just laugh.
Moments away from crying on the floor.

/ / / / / / / / / / / / / / / / / / / / / /

*I thought I was stronger.*
*Hit the gym, hit the punching bag.*
*He hit harder.*

*Lights flash in the dark part of my brain.*
*He stands over me in the middle of the ring.*
*Blood drips out of my mouth.*

*I thought I was calmer.*
*Took a deep breath, took my time.*
*He took more than that.*

# Summertime

It doesn't take a rocket scientist
to know I was happier in the summer.
Summertime heat, I claim I hate it.
I don't want to admit I was better for it.
I'd abandon my mental health
just to feel winter's cold breeze again.

Summer break, a fresh start.
I need a break from feeling broken.
I need to take time to get myself together.
Been trying to climb out of this pit,
the hole I dug myself into.
But I'd go back in a heartbeat,
turn the clock to the coldest night,
just to fall down that hill again.

It doesn't take a psyche degree
to know I was happier in the summer.
Summertime bliss, oh, how I miss it.
I don't want to admit I was at peace.
I'd forget everything I've learned
just to feel winter's cold breeze again.

# Bitter Taste

I'm not any happier now.
Thought I would be. I'm just bitter.
I don't feel any prettier. Just ugly inside.
I swore I used to smile more.
Now look at where things have gone.

Sucking on a raspberry candy,
the shell cracked and I was left with nothin'.
Do all sweet things lose their flavor?
And I ain't saying I'm proud of this.
I've got a bitter taste in my mouth.
Been trying to clean up my act,
clean up my speech,
but fuck if I ain't angry right now.

Ordered a drink in your honor.
Vodka mixed with spite.
Took one taste and spit it back in the cup.
I think I've finally had enough.
Got a laceration on my lip, so pour the salt in.
Been drowning myself in regret and self-pity.
Am I not a better person than that?
Cause I fear right now all I am is bitter.

I'm not any happier now.
Don't know why I ever thought differently.

# Letter From a Childhood Friend

*I found an unmarked envelope.*
*It was tucked underneath my window wipers.*
*The rain soaked the corner of the letter.*
*Smudged the signature at the bottom.*

Dear Joshua,

Word finally got around. Don't it always. I heard what you wrote, sounds like you've been using your words a little different these days. You told me you couldn't cry, didn't know how to talk about your emotions. Look at you now. I know my advice is unsolicited, but I've been meaning to write to you for a while now. You can keep my words or throw them away.

You used to complain about politics and the state of our country. I remember looking you in the eyes and asking you what you were going to do about it. I'm still waiting on things to change for the better. I admire your dedication to prayer, but God ain't saving this place anytime soon. If you ask me, it's up to us to make this world not such a living hell. And only then–when we can all quit being such evil freaks–might we finally see what Heaven looks like.

Why are you trying to hide amongst conservatives you think hate you? Take it from an old friend, living with a disguise will only ever make you lonely. No one hates you, and if they do, they can go and you-know-what themselves. If you could take a step back and see how much they care about you, if you could only have known how much I cared about you, maybe you would finally be able to let go of this self-loathing. You're a good person; I hope you can admit that to yourself. You can try to lie to them, but I know they see that same good in you.

I'll tell you what Jenna won't. She wants you to be happy, I want what's best for you. Stop daydreaming so much and start being present. Put your phone away, trust the words you're going to say. And I know you don't want to hear this, but that girl you're talking to isn't good for you. You tell me you love her, but I love you too much to let you do this to yourself. It's the pretty ones you have to look out for.

Soj told me you finished the first draft of your next book. He seemed concerned. Said you had been letting hurt feelings and the weight of everything collapse down on top of you. He brings up a fair point–and I know he cares about you–but he's no poet. What is poetry, if not a place where you can be honest with yourself? Let your sadness fill the pages, I've done the same. You're not childish for having emotions. No story is perfect, not mine, not yours, but they're all worth telling. If I could tell anything to younger me, I would want her to know as much.

You're beautiful, remember that. I don't care if you wear makeup or decide to go weeks without shaving. Don't ever let your insecurities take up the space where your smile is. I've been there. Plenty. Body dysmorphia is a bitch. Missing meals, showering three times a day, chemicals on my skin, none of it made the nightmare go away.

I read what you wrote about me. I may not have known how to say it back then, but your friendship meant the world to me. We were just kids, both of still trying to learn what it even means to love one another. Hell, I didn't even know how to love myself back then. And I think that showed in every relationship I ever had. It took breaking that trauma for me to truly fall in love. So, take it from me, when I say, "I love you," it still means something. The scars you draw aren't what heal you, it's learning to let go of the pain.

Until our next dance, take care of yourself, please. And hey, at least you know I love you.

with love,

# The Past I Can't Find

Tattoos and eyeliner.
That's the way I remember you.
Never thought we would say goodbye.
Said you didn't have a reason to stay,
but you were mine.

Let's get drunk and write shitty poems.
Cry together like only two friends can.

We thought we were so smart back then.
And maybe we were,
but I feel stupid for letting you go.
People will ask me what my career goals are.
It's the day you hear one of my songs on the radio.
When you find a copy of this on a bookstore shelf.

Conversations about sex and religion.
Talking through the trauma forced upon us.
I don't miss teenage angst or my high school days,
but damnit, I miss sharing those years with you.

I still pray I'll see you at church again.
You and I sharing a pew like the old days.
I know you don't believe in God,
but you always believed in me.
Even when I didn't, you loved me.

# August

If I had been born in August
what would my mother have named me?
If I had been born at the end of summer
would I be able to see myself more clearly?

How would the seasons have changed?
The paint in my eyes on my ninth birthday.
My sister and I trading secrets.
Being confused at my first slumber party.
Would my childhood friends have stayed the same?
Desperately praying on my fourteenth birthday.
Going on dates for all the wrong reasons.
Crying the first time I broke their rules.

If I had been born in August
what would my mother have named me?
If I was born in purple linen
would I be more precious than your jewels?
Dressed in strength and dignity, no fear of the snow.
A smile so warm and caring, reaping what I sow.

If I had been born on a rainy day
would I still be a writer and teacher?
If I had been born on a beautiful day
would I have stayed or walked away?

If I had been born in August
what would my mother have named me?
If I had been born at the end of summer
would I be able to see myself more clearly?

# Thrift Store

Unwanted to everyone else,
but in this place I feel loved.
No judgement, no expectations,
no need to match my complexion
to the world's understanding.

Shopping for another metaphor,
I'll take it used.
It's everything I ever wanted.
Dirty picture frames to hold a faded image.
Old cocktail glasses to fill with dated liquor.
And while the clothes are cheap,
the price to wear it is still out of reach.

Unwanted to everyone else,
but in this place I feel loved.
No judgment, no expectations,
no need to match my complexion
to the world's understanding.

Under the dingy lights and musky smell,
the future feels brighter than ever.
The hope of a second chance,
to be loved, to be held close.
To find someone who sees my beauty,
not just the threads of the past.
And one day that dream may just come true.

# Writing This Didn't Make Me Feel Better

I've been dreaming of telling you off.
To get the last word in, to finally win.
I'm not proud of the fact that I still let you get to my head.
You were a dream I once had,
now I want to be your nightmare.

In the fictional scenario where I see you again,
I'll finally stand up to you. I should have long ago.
Tell you to leave me alone. Don't ever touch me.
I could finally look you in the eye and tell you to fuck off.
Prove to my friends you don't control me.

You always made me out to be the jerk,
so I might as well give you some credibility.
I have a love-hate relationship with the way
you say my name. It can make my day.
You can ruin my night.

I want to tell you off.
I want to get the last word in, I want to finally win.
I want closure, I want the satisfaction, I want you to know.
Know how much you meant to me,
and that the things you said to me hurt.

*A part of me wants to hurt you back,*
*and I hate myself every time I admit it.*
*I'm sorry. I wish I was better than this.*

# On the Day

On the day I can't write a song,
I'll go for a quiet drive instead.
Pondering all the questions I want to ask life,
wait in silence for her answer.
And I'll wait a while,
and that wait will eventually turn to poetry.

On the day we're friends again,
I'll apologize for the time lost to hurt feelings.
It's a pity the way we learned to hold a grudge.
For the mean things needlessly said,
even more for the things left unsaid.
Once upon a time we were actually friends.
Now I'm sitting here, not so sure anymore.
Hating the way love turns to resentment.

On the day when I let my trauma live in peace,
I'll walk out those doors for the last time.
I've been scared to leave for so long,
worried of what you'd say,
worried about who I've become.
And maybe I just didn't want to acknowledge
the relationship we've fostered is a toxic one.
But feeling pain doesn't make you weak,
it's ignoring it that will kill you.

On the day the flowers blossom,
I'll understand the beauty of these days.
The story I unknowingly have been writing.

# Raspberry Tootsie Pop

Snow and ice on the sidewalk.
Raspberry Tootsie Pop in my mouth.
Walking to nowhere. Praying to no one.
God, I hope you hear me, but I'm not so sure.

Walk one block, nearly slip and fall.
A smart man would turn around.
Obviously that's not what I do.

The first time I said I love you to a girl I was lying.
I wonder if she knew at the time.
The first time I realized I was in love it hurt my eyes.
I think I always knew it would.
In about eight months this snow will thaw.
On that day I'll be happy again, but oh God,
what about right now?

Snow and ice on the sidewalk.
Raspberry Tootsie Pop in my mouth.
Walking to nowhere. Praying to my God.
Despite my wishes, a prayer I won't soon forget.

Walk for three miles, clearly lost in song.
A wise man would get some rest.
Obviously that's not what I do.

As I recount the memories like quarters,
I resound on a few regrets,
wishing I didn't spend so much time trying to
find rhymes for songs I would never finish.
These tears would freeze into ink,
the stories that would break me apart,
until I learned to reshape what they meant.

Snow and ice on the sidewalk.
Raspberry Tootsie Pop in my mouth.
Walking to nowhere. Praying on my doorsteps.
I won't leave here, not until these words are heard.

# Last Night She Left Me

Jenna invited me to join her for dinner on Friday. I agreed, though I knew I had better things to do.

We both arrived early, typical of the each of us. She is all dressed up, every detail of her outfit thought out. I just wear an undershirt and jeans.

The two of us catch up for a little bit. I retell of my friends and I's hijinks. She blushes while telling me about the girl she's been dating. She sounds amazing. I'm happy for you.

She hardly touches her meal. I say to her, you should eat more. She gives me a smirk. *"Who do you think I learned this from?"*

*"At the end of the day, I simply want to be healthy and pretty. Just not in that order."* I look at my unfinished plate and sigh.

The conversation ebbs and flows. We talk of politics, music, sports, and more. She asks me about my family.

When I tell her they're all doing well her eyes well up. *"I'm glad to hear,"* she replies. A pain hidden within her sight.

She looks to the sky with a smile. *"Y'know, I don't regret a thing. I just regret this is the way things had to go."* I nod my head, trying to understand, but I'll be damned if I do.

There's a silence as we both search for what to say next. No tension, only a sense of longing in the air. One I know all too well.

Do you believe God is good, I ask her. Because some days when I look at the world, I'm not so sure anymore.

*"There's no stronger feeling I've ever felt than love. So, if God's real, and I believe so, then I know that love must point back to him."*

Then why do I feel like there's something missing in me? Why can't I find the love pointing at me? I say I agree with her, keeping these thoughts to myself.

I tell her I fixed up my old scooter; she teases me about my time hopping shenanigans. *"Do the memories haunt or comfort you?"*

A bit of both, I'd say. The more time that goes by, the more distance I feel I've let roll by. Not that I'm complaining, but the more memories I collect, the more I let the old ones go.

I see a wave of dread beginning to set on her face, as if she already knows the answer to the question about to be asked. *"Do you still see me when you travel to the future?"*

I look out at the trees in the distance, trying to avoid making eye contact. I tell her no.

I try to convince her she still means so much to me. She interrupts me. *"Don't do that. Please. I just need some space, okay?"*

*"I love you,"* she said, holding back the tears. The same ones that reflected the moonlight in her eyes. "I just hope you can learn to love yourself."

I'm trying. Just give me a little more time. Show me how you did it, tell me all the reasons you love me.

She shook her head silently. Her hands reached for mine. She held them and smiled sadly. *"I need to go."*

Don't leave, I told her half-heartedly. I need you still. I want to be you. I don't think she believed me.

*"Joshua, we deserve to be happy with who we are. So, go and be happy. And if we ever cross paths again, don't be a stranger."*

She leaned in and kissed me on the cheek. It felt cold. She walked away, crying the whole way. I stood there, feeling nothing at all.

Her imagery became imaginary. What she meant to me was just a memory.

# Eros and Philautia

*Okay, so, this was one of the last poems I wrote for this book. Call it a bit of an editorial note.*

I met her on a walk.
She was absolutely gorgeous.
What I imagine an angel would look like.
But by God, I've only ever been human.

I'm better with a pen than a paintbrush,
but I bought a sketchbook just to draw her eye.
With every line she was on my mind.
If I could write a story it would be in her voice.
Now I got a box of her clothes,
wish I had somewhere to wear them to.

My imaginary girl,
life is funny, the timing is always crazy,
around that time I met someone
who I saw something real in.
Said I wouldn't change myself for her.
I did anyway, for the better I like to think.

I knew a girl whom I had a crush on.
I thought I knew a lot,
but with her I had to rethink everything.
Poetry, prayer, and pure intentions.
'Of all God's daughters, what is it
about you that I find so beautiful?'

The thing I remember the best about her
was the way I didn't hate myself when she was around.
I hope she knows how much that meant to me.
'And I know you were no angel,
but you're just as gorgeous to me.
Even your imperfections are pretty to me,
because they remind me of mine.'

There are topics I know to not talk about.
Queer identity. Sex and whatnot.
The hurt caused by religion and good intentions.
The places to tread lightly, keep my little mouth shut.
I know not to say, "I love you."
Because there are truths better kept to myself.

Poems on my desktop that won't ever see the light of day.
About me, about her, about everything.
Love, identity, and the confusion of the two.
She was everything I wanted to be.
And she left. But something stayed with me.

Would have changed everything for her.
Now I just want to know how her story goes.
Where did she go after walking away?
Did she ever buy that lavender dress?
Did she ever make amends with her family?
Did she cry the first time like she thought she would?
Did she find God in the life she went on to make?

I just want to know how my story will go.
Do I ever love myself like I did with her?

## chapter vi

# construction at the junction of i-35 and highway 9

another innocent civilian marked dead.
no need for a game of clue,
they were murdered in the daylight.
i'll make a stop by the casino tonight,
gamble my life on a promise never kept,
lose all my money for a conman's debt.
call it a protest, call it terrorism,
throw a red flag and challenge the call.
i read the red plan, a bullet in the chamber,
promote all your pawns to protect the king.
bow down and worship his mighty ring,
or spin the cylinder and pull the trigger.

# Ruler of This Land

If I were ruler of this land,
first I would kill all the artists.
I would criminalize comedy.
No one is allowed to be funnier than I am.
The media will advertise my threats as jokes
and the people won't be the wiser.

I've got a plan for this nation.
A plan that has your best interest at heart.
Freedom is too overwhelming, let me do the thinking.
Trust me, obey me, follow me,
and I'll make your name great in heaven.

If I were ruler of this land,
I would find all the lonely young men,
angry at the world, something to prove,
and tell them how much I love them.
All they have to do to earn my respect
is put on a mask, protect these lands.
Go and clean the streets for me.

If I were ruler of this land,
I would stand and pray at the street corners,
prove to them that I'm a religious man.
The people need to know I'm on their team.
I'm one of great faith, so put yours in me.
I'll keep all the money in my pockets,
but give every last thought and prayer to you.

If I were ruler of this land,
I would ensure a bright future for us all
by raising new rules on who will raise our children.
Make sure the next generation is birthed
by only the purest, most motherly women,
fathered by only the fittest, most qualified men.
Those with a certain shine about them.

I've got a plan for this nation.
A plan that has your best interest at heart.
Freedom is too overwhelming, let me do the thinking.
Trust me, obey me, follow me,
and I'll make your name great in heaven.

If I were ruler of this land,
I would give the police more weapons,
all I ask in exchange is their loyalty.
Remind them that a protest is only a
brick away from a threat to the state.
And I'll always throw the first stone
if it gives a precedent to lock up the terrorists.

If I were ruler of this land,
I would let my own friends die as martyrs,
use their death as a rallying cry,
calling for vengeance while the body is still warm.
Point the people to the real enemy, Satan and his friends.
And when the devil runs his course,
I'll find a new people to demonize.

If I were ruler of this land,
I would teach the children everything
they need to know to serve in this country.
No more indoctrination, no more sexual deviancy,
no more guilt in our nation's history.
It's time to remove fear from the curriculum.
Why worry these kids with learning about
the holocaust and such things?
There's no need to spoil the ending.

If I were ruler of this beautiful, deeply troubled land,
first I would kill all the artists.

# Protest #1

*BLM March (c. 2020)*

Silvia showed me the photos on her phone.
She said, "I took this picture about ten minutes
before the police arrived."
And there she bravely stood, best dressed for a protest.
Jet black eyeliner, an ACAB facemask,
and her ripped-up slate hoodie.
"Now's the time to stand up. Let them see you."

Hey writer boy, you ain't staying quiet now.
Wear your best clothes and let's walk arm in arm.
One, two, a thousand in the streets.
She told me, "Our rights are taken when we don't fight."

Two teenagers sitting in a Dairy Queen parking lot.
I talked about revolution and she talked of real change.
"Democracy, community, and poetry," she said,
"These are the things that are important to me."
She had been there that day, while I had stayed home.
I told her I admire her conviction.
I asked her if speaking out was a scary thing.
She sighed deeply, "I can't stay silent forever, can I?"
Tear gas fell from the skyline.
She grasped the sleeve of her jacket.
"Joshua, we're only as free as the least of us.
If we allow the abuse of the blue man to stand,
then how will we ever learn to stand up for ourselves?"

Hey writer boy, you ain't staying quiet now.
Wear your best clothes and let's walk arm in arm.
One, two, a thousand in the streets.
She told me, "Even on the dark nights life is worth the fight."

# Parade in the Streets

There's going to be a parade in the streets!
I'm sorry you'll have to miss it,
but sleep easy knowing we're all celebrating.
Men hugging, women crying tears of joy.
There's going to be a parade in the streets!

Open the champagne bottle!
Piss on the pasture side!
Best bathroom in town!
Today's a day worth remembering,
because we'll never forget what you did.

There's going to be a parade in the streets!
I'm sorry you'll have to miss it,
but sleep easy knowing we're all celebrating.
Men hugging, women crying tears of joy.
There's going to be a parade in the streets!

Walking down Jones Avenue
is a girl with a smile on her face,
her happy stare tells more than enough.
There's going to be a celebration!
No need for elaboration.
There's going to be a party in the nation!
A day of liberation.

There's going to be a parade in the streets!
All because of you.

# Kid at the Gym

The kid over there, you see him?
Scrawny arms, messy hair, something to prove.
He's here every day.
Watches everyone else in silence.
They're all stronger. They're all prettier.
He envies them. He hates them.

The kid over there, you see him?
The bar fell on him. Everyone stared, no one helped.
He just wants them to see him.
Now he hides in the corner, keeps to himself.
Slowly his strength grows along with hatred.
Vows that the people here will notice him one day.

The kid over there, you see him?
He bought a pair of gloves. Took them downtown.
Found the place where the rejected and dejected go.
When he stepped in the cage he finally felt free.
Everyone laughed at him, they thought he was a joke.
Tell that to the man lying in a pool of his own blood.

The kid over there, you see him?
The scars covering his arms are his own doing.
He wears a mask, the life in his eyes died long ago.
Will throw a punch without a word said.
Beaten countless, had them clinging to their lives.
I met him in the ring once; never been punched harder.

The kid over there, you see him?
I recognize him.
He hides his loneliness under a mask.
He tries to replace anxiety with anger.
He is scared the world will hurt him.
He lets his own insecurities cloud his mind.
He hates who he is.
Thinks the only way he'll ever feel safe
is if he burns the entire world to an ash.
The kid over there, lingering in my shadow,
hiding in the reflections, I recognize him.

# Winter Wonderland

Woke up to a frozen wasteland.
A cold chill creeping down my spine.
Watch the scurrying feet of
frightened little snow mice.
Consequences purge like frostbite.
Wear a mask and hood to protect yourself.
No fingerprints, no evidence,
death by icicle.
But all ice melts eventually.
And crime is crime,
I don't care what the order was.
The snow will dry again one day,
revealing a field of lilies and lies.

# Agent Jeff

The child of a single mother.
Grew up in the nineties. Had a pet dog named Rosie.
Back then life was good according to him.
Back before it all went to shit.
Rosie passed away and the world passed him by.
More and more people moved to his town,
they drove up the cost of homes, forcing his mom out.
He watched his opportunities go to kids he never met.
They laughed at him, wagged their fingers in his face.
Never had a lucky break in his life,
he had to fight for everything.
We'll see who's laughing now,
now that he's the one wagging a gun.

Agent Jeff, Immigrant and Customs Enforcement officer.
He beat a brown man last week.
Kidnapped a baby straight from their mother's arms.
Maced a student. Kicked a protestor.
Then shot your neighbor for objecting the peace.

He remembers the TV screen
while he got his braces tightened,
the second tower falling from the skyline.
He was terrified, never felt smaller inside.
Only twelve at the time, his country in a panic.
He was angry at the people who hated his way of life.
Swore he would get his vengeance.
Got his first real job in '08, lost it 8 days later.
Started looking for work, bounced around for years.
Never held a steady career. Wished he had never been born.
Flunked med school. Was kicked out of the police academy.
His life was in the balance when he refused any help,
turned to a substance that told him he was fine,
drank himself to sleep every night for years to come.

Agent Jeff, Immigrant and Customs Enforcement officer.
He beat a brown man last week.
Kidnapped a baby straight from their mother's arms.
Maced a student. Kicked a protestor.
Then shot your neighbor for objecting the peace.

Got married young to a woman he hates.
She's just as bitter, enables his hateful actions.
Has no respect for him, her and her secret affair.
And he can't express himself without violence.
Put himself in debt to raise a family he didn't want.
He was ready for a change, voted red in '16,
found a man who told him his anger was justified.
Started blaming his problems on everyone but himself.
Watches news reels on his phone,
the clips from the talking heads and podcast bros.
His skin burns, crooked teeth gnashing.
He's not responsible. They are. This is their fault.
The reason he doesn't know a thing about his own children.
The reason his wife won't even touch him anymore.
The reason his mother died of a disease he thought was fake.
The reason the country he loves is falling apart.

Agent Jeff, Immigrant and Customs Enforcement officer.
He beat a brown man last week.
Kidnapped a baby straight from their mother's arms.
Maced a student. Kicked a protestor.
Then shot your neighbor for objecting the peace.

Thought he could right the wrongs of his life.
Now the world hates him.
Has trouble sleeping at night, miserable all the time.
No sympathy from his enemies, even less from his friends.
But he'll still say it's not his fault.
He was just listening to what he was told.

# Antifascists

They stormed the beaches of Normandy.
They decrypted signals before Midway.
They hid families in their own homes.
Call them heroes. Call them patriots.
Call them what they are: Antifascists.

Pilecki stepped foot where no free man would.
The Schindlers spent their fortune to pardon workers.
Doss repeatedly risked his life to save another.
Gut hid and sheltered the lives of the innocent.
The Six Triple Eight gave millions a reason to keep fighting.
Murphy. Khan. Sugihara. Wallenberg.
The names of them all would fill this page.
Countless more whose stories we will never know.

They stormed the beaches of Normandy.
They decrypted signals before Midway.
They hid families in their own homes.
Call them heroes. Call them patriots.
Call them what they are: Antifascists.

The Nazis deported the people not like them.
Separated children from their families
in the name of national security.
Infiltrated the courts, put their word above the law.
Sent the police against their own citizens, locking up
trade unionists, religious dissenters, and students alike.
Liars. Killers. Bullies.
There's no need to clarify, they were the bad guys.

So, as I live, and as all do, one day die,
I'll speak out against fascism and hate.
And if you don't like that, just you wait,
the history books will write your name in shame.
Our freedom is taken when we remain silent.
Lives are lost when we're content to be bystanders.

# Protest #2

*Pride Parade (c. 2024)*

Jenna dragged me by the arm down Main Street.
She said, "C'mon, let's go! The parade will
start any moment."
And there she calmly stood, best dressed for a protest.
A pair of cobalt jeans, pink crop top,
and her sparkling blueberry lipstick.
"Now's the time to stand up. Let them see you."

Hey writer boy, you ain't staying quiet now.
Wear your best clothes and let's go celebrate.
One, two, a thousand in the streets.
She told me, "Love is love and what you make of it."

Two hopeless romantics wanting to be seen.
We argued about which girls here go which way.
"Faith, a loving hug, and being pretty," she said,
"These are the things that are important to me."
She was smiling the whole time, while I hid behind her.
I told her I don't belong here. She laughed at me.
I asked her if she thought we would ever find love.
I mean, someone who loves who we really are.
Confetti rained from the clouds.
She grabbed my hand and held it to her heart.
"Joshua, I honestly don't know.
But if you'll love me,
then I know there's someone who will feel the same."

Hey writer boy, you ain't staying quiet now.
Wear your best clothes and let's go celebrate.
One, two, a thousand in the streets.
She told me, "They can't take who we are from us."

# No Child Left Behind

No child left behind. We Left them all.
In pursuit of what we want.
Happiness. Call it freedom.
No child left behind. We Left them all.
Life and liberty. Power and cash.
No child left behind. We Left them all.

Guns and the economy.
We invest in the stocks
but won't invest in our future.
Won't protect their hearts.
*(Or other vital organs)*
Let them fight for the top spot.
Only a few make it through,
the rest will serve the best.

Takes a village to raise a little one.
Only takes one to turn them away.
The best lesson they're taught
is that life isn't necessarily fair.
*(Sharing stops after the recess bell)*
Change the requirements for success.
Teach them a system of tests
that'll fill them with anxiety and stress.

It might be bullshit. But we profit.
Think about the children. But don't think too long.

No child left behind. We Left them all.
In pursuit of what we want.
Happiness. Call it freedom.
No child left behind. We Left them all.
Life and liberty. Power and cash.
No child left behind. We Left them all.

Tell them to dream big.
Crush those dreams while they sleep.
Punish them for learning,
ridicule the questions they ask.
*(Blame them if the math doesn't add up)*
When they talk, say, 'Shut up.'
They're not humans, they're problems.
So, they better not get in our way.

Here's the report card.
Give them an A for their anxiety.
Give them a B for the bullshit.
Give them a C for the censorship.
Give them a slap on the face and call it a life lesson.
Give them an F you.

Fire drills and emergencies.
Keep the kids in a straight line.
There's only right and wrong.
Every child must walk the same way.
*(It's for their safety, mind you)*
Step out a line, you become the target.
When the guns come to show and tell
they'll be the first shot, dead on the spot.

It might be bullshit. But we profit.
Think about the children. But don't think too long.

No child left behind. We Left them all.
In pursuit of what we want.
Happiness. Call it freedom.
No child left behind. We Left them all.
Life and liberty. Power and cash.
No child left behind.

# The Weeping of the Childless

*"A voice was heard in Ramah, weeping and loud lamentation,*
*Rachel weeping for her children; she refused to be comforted,*
*because they are no more."* -*Jeremiah 3:15*

Ambulance sirens sound into the late evening.
The sky is hazy and faint.
They're gone. A town taken by tragedy.
No more can you hear them laugh, running around without a care.
They're gone. A home broken by treachery.
They spent their last minute screaming, running around in fear.
They're gone. What have we done?

It's the weeping of the childless,
the sorrow, pain, and bitterness.
The night has never felt this dark.
Tears turn cemetery dirt to mud
and blood-stained clothes are left unwashed.
For tonight will live and love will die.

Welcome to the land of the free, where violence is our tyranny.
Suffering is just the price we pay.
I don't know what's it like to lose everything.
Everything you love. Everything that keeps you going.
Everything in the world. They do. And I just pray I never will.

Y'know on Friday night they were going to order a pizza,
stay up late, watch a movie, it would've been great.
Now dad comforts mom, trying to hide the heartbreak
that you and I cannot even imagine.
Instead on Friday they planned the funeral
that we sent out the invitation for,
because our weapons just meant more.

It's the weeping of the childless,
the sorrow, pain, and bitterness.
The night has never felt this dark.
Tears turn cemetery dirt to mud
and blood-stained clothes are left unwashed.
For tonight will live and love will die.

It's a pain I can't imagine.
A cross none of us are willing to bear.
Brother, the necklace around your throat,
the one about the death of your savior;
did Jesus die so you can live?
What would he say when we've killed
the only innocence left inside any of us.

A mother weeps the night, she weeps the day.
Pain in every second and anger in every heartbeat.
Her husband and her fight and scream,
they miss the life they had,
the one where love was theirs.
We keep the bullets sounding in the streets.
War is fought with blood; don't you get it?
This is our right. The right to live and the right to die.

She holds a gun in her hand.
Thinking about that day again.
She just wants to see her babies again.
Kiss them on the cheek again.
She holds a gun in her hand.
All it took was a few stray bullets.
It was our careless refusal to act.
We let a killer on the loose.
She holds a gun in her hand.
Knowing she can see them in Heaven.
Why is the world so empty?
Can't she just be happy?!

It's the weeping of the childless,
the sorrow, pain, and bitterness!
The night has never felt this dark.
Tears turn cemetery dirt to mud
and blood-stained clothes are left unwashed.
For tonight will live and love will die.
It's the weeping of the childless,
the pain, the shame, the dying breath.

*"Little children, let us not love in word or talk but in deed and truth."* Your blood was a part of our war. No more.

# God, Welcome to America

What would God say?
If he knew you and I hated each other.
We could be friends, we could kiss.
We could kiss all our problems away.
But no, we bicker like two toddlers.

What would God say?
To all the fascists at the altar.
Lighting the fire of their own damnation,
spreading flames like a disease of the heart.
And I too should be damned for any sin
said in my Lord's name that I fail to shame.

What would God say?
When he sees the field of tombstones.
The young girls bleeding for their abusers.
There are guns and roses behind the baptismal.
For the party we hold in our church
is the party of bullets and pro-life signs.
Men who build ivory idols on land they've stolen.
The Bible is held up by rapists and murderers.
They may prey, lay their hands on the innocent.
We nail a cross to the back of children,
send them off to die for what we call freedom.

What would God say?
If we welcomed him to America.

# Protest #3

*No Kings Protest (c. 2026)*

Soj held the pamphlets, I carried the poster board.
He said, “Look at the turnout. The sky may be gray,
but my friend, today is looking a little brighter.”
And there he proudly stood, best dressed for a protest.
A windbreaker, ‘Protect Trans Kids’ shirt,
and his ‘25 OKC Thunder cap.
“Now’s the time to stand up. Let them see you.”

Hey writer boy, you ain’t staying quiet now.
Wear your best clothes and let’s go protest.
One, two, a thousand in the streets.
He told me, “There’s still hope for our country yet.”

Two friends talking with the people on the sidewalk.
We listened to the stories that brought them here.
“Clear skies, my friends, and being free,” we both said,
“These are the things that are important to me.”
He would explain the logistics, while I shouted rhetoric.
I told him that as I won’t serve a king a day I’m alive.
I asked him if he thought we could actually win.
He pointed to the crowd, “We have to try, don’t we?”
Rain drizzled from the Heavens.
He picked up a sign a held it high above his head.
“Joshua, the worst thing we can do is stay inside.
If we’re there for each other,
then no matter what happens we won’t be alone.”

Hey writer boy, you ain’t staying quiet now.
Wear your best clothes and let’s go protest.
One, two, a thousand in the streets.
He told me, “Somebody has to be the change in the world.”

# United People (Worth a Dime)

Penny pinching in the Walmart parking lot.
Budgeting with a toothpick and some blood.
Praying to the Lord for good health,
cause the bill will be a death sentence.

Another CEO died yesterday.
I tried to feel some sympathy,
but my heart has too many maladies.
If only I could afford my premium.
We're all the same. All want a good life.
But can't afford the subscription.
The price to be happy is too high,
maybe you can buy it with ads.

Ninety-nine rats fighting for one piece of cheese,
while one rodent lives in a mansion of Brie.

Divided we aren't worth a dime.
Only when united will they give a damn.
Divided we aren't worth a dime.
Only when united will they give a damn.

Save enough money so you
can afford to be sick one day.
Maybe someday we'll retire from our second jobs.
If only you worked harder.
Forty hours, that's rookie numbers.
Don't have the time or money for a family.
Your boss needs you to make him an extra dollar,
then you can at least buy yourself a nice dinner.

United Health is a cancer. But they'll deny that claim too.
Bandages make the drug company money, not cures.
Lockheed execs get hard watching tapes of war.
Drone strikes are a great business opportunity.
The electric company won't give you a single notice.
They can always take what they so graciously gave us.
So, check left, check right, before you cross the street.
It ain't the people on the sidewalk taking your money.
Those potholes are same ones I drive upon.
We've got the numbers and that terrifies them.

Ninety-nine pigeons fighting for the last crumb,
while one vulture waits for what they will become.

Divided we aren't worth a dime.
Only when united will they give a damn.
Divided we aren't worth a dime.
Only when united will they give a damn.

# Angry at the World

I felt so lonely, so scared of the little things,
back in those days when I was angry at the world.

I was lied to as a kid,
I was promised things would work out,
and when I realized that was never true,
I took it out on all of you.
It was easier to blame everyone else
then realize I was no less human than the rest.

I felt so lonely, so scared of the little things,
back in those days when I was angry at the world.

It's no excuse, but I was confused.
Confused to why people treat each other so badly,
when we all have more in common than not.
And that was a scary thought.
I'm still trying to understand what I preach.
Doing my best to live up to the words I teach.

I felt so lonely, so scared of the little things,
back in those days when I was angry at the world.

I was rightly mad at the state of things,
but I made little effort to be the change.
Learned the hard way negativity doesn't help out,
it just fills you with misery and self-doubt.
The world wasn't better off for my complaining.
I found living in that state was far too draining.

I felt so lonely, so scared of the little things,
back in those days when I was angry at the world.

All alone. No one listening.
Spouting angry rants.
The ramblings of a scared teenager.
All alone. Afraid of the world.
Felt like no one understood.
I think we all feel that way sometimes.
All alone. Mad and a little sad.
It took putting that anger away
to realize seclusion is no way to live life.

I felt so lonely, so scared of the little things,
back in those days when I was angry at the world.

chapter vii

# outsourcing your self-respect is a bit of an oxymoron

i've changed as a person.
my aunt noticed it, my friends said as much.
i'm not that scared little kid anymore.
more so, i finally feel like a real person.
and with that comes its own problems.
my favorite poem is in this chapter.
you reminded me people can be friendly.
tell me you love- well, tell me you love-
you proved to me i'm worth something.
tell me you love- well, tell me you love-
and if you can give me a reason to smile,
shouldn't i be able to find a reason in me too?

# Emotional Disorder

And the secret is I want the attention.
I won't go to the doctor,
I don't want to fix the issue.
Because when my friends ask if I'm okay
it makes me feel seen.
I don't need to be told to eat and sleep more,
I just want to know I'm loved.
And before you try to feel bad for me,
just know I already know what's wrong with that.

Skipped lunch on Wednesday.
Said I'd eat something a little later,
then pretended to forget.
I'm addicted to the feeling I get
when you're proud of me for eating a full meal.
It doesn't happen much,
I wouldn't want to overdo a good thing.

Shaking and clearly disassociating,
waiting for you to comfort me.
If you love me at my worst
then I never have to be at my best.

If you love me
then I never have to love myself.

# Hear You Say

I want to hear you say to me, "You're so smart."
Tell me I'm pretty. Tell me I'm beautiful.
I just lie in wait till you say, "You're so amazing."
Tell me I'm a good friend. Tell me you love me.

I use myself as the punchline in a joke,
but self-deprecation never makes anyone laugh.
Why do I think saying I don't like myself
will convince you that you should?
I beat myself up because I want you to comfort me.
I lie, hoping you'll call me out on it.

Tell me you noticed all the small things I did for you.
Let me know that you see me trying my hardest.
The words fall flat in the bathroom mirror.
I need to hear it from you. Do you love me?
Just say you do. Please, I need this from you.

I keep tearing myself down
just so you can build me up again.

I want to hear you say to me, "You're so sweet."
Tell me I'm pretty. Tell me I'm beautiful.
I just lie in wait till you say, "You're so amazing."
Tell me I'm a good friend. Tell me you love me.

I just want to hear you say, "You're a good person."
I've been trying. I really have.

## Sarcastic Sorry

I'm sorry. Really.
I mean it this time.
I'm sorry I'm not perfect.
I'm sorry that your feelings are hurt.
I apologize for not being good enough.
I should have tried a little harder, shouldn't I have.
If only I was better with my words.
Maybe then people would read my books.

I'm sorry I can't read your mind.
I'm sorry that you don't like it when I speak up for myself.
Next time I'll stay quiet.
Apparently silence sounds better than my voice,
it's my fault for not realizing that sooner.
Sorry about that.

I'm sorry I ever listened to begin with.
I'm sorry I wasted my time here.
I'm sorry for ever giving you the time of day.
I won't make that mistake again.

And I'm sorry,
sorry for...
The way I pathologize the past.
The way I villainize other people.
I'm sorry for not calling.
I'm sorry for being a bother.
And I'm sorry that I can't differentiate between the two.
I apologize for playing the victim.
I apologize for not acknowledging the hurtful things I say.
Most of all, I'm sorry that I'm still holding on to this.
It's not fair to you. It's not fair to me.
So, I'm sorry. Really.

# Forgiveness

Jesus said to forgive before you stand to pray.
Leave your offering to reconcile.
And this is the part where I get caught up,
say the verse don't apply to my songs.
But I did the math, I get four hundred and ninety tries
to show compassion instead of hold a grudge.
Finally show grace to the one person I don't want to.

I want to forgive myself.
For all the shit I hold on to.
Remember those hateful things I said?
I said I'm sorry. Now I want to forgive.
I may not forget, but I'll let go,
leave behind my worst tendencies.

Can forgive the friend who stays by my side.
Show grace if you bat your pretty eyes.
Now when I look down at my hands
I want to be able to do the same.
God hear me, God forgive me,
because I don't know if I know how to.

I want to forgive myself.
For all the fault I pin to my name.
Remember the criticism I kept shouting?
I said I'm sorry. Now I want to forgive.
I may not forget, but I'll let go,
leave behind my worst tendencies.

God hear me, God forgive me,
because I don't know if I know how to.

# Hide and Seek

You can look inside.
You can look outside.
You can look wherever you like.
You can look inside.
You can look outside.
You can look wherever you like.

You won't find me.
You won't find what you're looking for.
So cry about it. But you won't find me.

You can fall in love.
You can be praised.
You can make money.
But you won't find me.
You can raise a family.
You can rule over everyone.
You can win the game.
But I'm playing by a different set of rules.

You can look inside.
You can look outside.
You can look wherever you like.
You can look inside.
You can look outside.
You can look wherever you like.

Chase your dream. Be who you want to be.
You won't find me.
Check under the couch cushion.
Look behind the cabinet.
Search around in the closet.
You won't find me.
You won't find what you're looking for.

# You Deserve

Girl, you deserve the world.
You deserve to be heard.
You deserve so much better,
better than what you've been told.

I almost cried when I overheard what you said,
it damn near broke my heart.
What makes you think that this is okay?
You deserve to be the greatest thing in someone's life.
More than just a lonely wife.

Honey, I know this will hurt like hell.
But don't let yourself play second fiddle
in your own story.
That's not the girl I know.
The one I swore would make a difference.
Nothing in this life or the next will ever stop you.

Don't think you have to sell your soul to be loved,
I know that feeling all too well.
That path won't lead you anywhere.
No amount of lying to yourself,
drinking, prayer, or compromise will change that.

And you can try to figure it out,
because loving someone is worth it.
But love isn't always enough
to keep things going.
Wish someone told me that sooner.

Girl, you deserve the world.
You deserve to be heard.
You deserve so much better,
better than what you've been told.

# Get Up

My eyes pop open. Where am I?
There's a ringing in my ears.
Every inch–from head to toe–hurts.

This is our fourth fight.
He's won every time.
I keep saying I'm strong enough,
this will be the time I take down Cloudy Eye.
Hff, I don't know why I bother.

My eyes pop open. Where am I?
There's a ringing in my ears.
Every inch–from head to toe–hurts.

This was the fourth night.
Hardly got any rest.
I keep saying I'm okay,
this will be the day I wake with a smile.
Hff, I don't know why I bother.

I hear Soj calling from the sideline.
*Get up.* I don't want to.
*Get up.* Just let me stay here, please.
*Get up.* What's the point?
*Get up.* I'll just end up here again.
*Get up.* Why keep trying?
*Get up.* Nothing good is waiting for me.
I'm just going turn over and stay here.
*Joshua, get the fuck up!*

I stare at the ceiling. Take it one breath at a time.
Move one muscle than another.
Hand. Hand. Foot. Foot. I stand up in a base.

Alright, I'm fine. Ready for round five?

# Plausible Deniability

Sitting in the workshop is a punk (derogatory) writer.
Is it intentional or incompetence that the artist
left the names anonymous?
A misdirection for the readers' discretion.
It comes across as malicious and fictitious,
the underlying fear of the contentious.

I'm retelling stories that may sound familiar.
Changing a few words, trying to not offend anyone.
I said this would be my most personal book yet,
but I've made up fake people to tell it.
The figments of my imagination
are nothing more than reflections of my friendships.

I said I wouldn't get controversial,
is that because the Christian socialist shtick got old?
I promised to not swear,
but that went out the window chapters ago.
I refuse to be personal,
is that because I don't like who that person is?

Write a book that tells the story you've created.
Change enough to veil the connections to real life.
Rewrite and rewrite to avoid what's obvious.
Guise your memories and feelings between the lines.
So, when I hand you the finished book
you can ask me about the characters
and I can tell you they're imaginary.
It gives me a sense of plausible deniability
when they ask who 'you' stands for.
Because I don't know any other way to say I love you.

# A Game of Twenty-One

You wanna play a game of 1-on-1?

*Sure. First to 21.*
*You check me in.*

'He dribbles past me, I make a desperate attempt at a block, but he lays it right in. I miss seven shots before I make my first one.'

Soj, I finally took your advice.
Kept my eyes up, took a deep breath first.
And I finally said sorry.
Even more so, I finally let go.

'I glance up at the rim. I inhale, step back, and let the ball go. Watch it gently fall through the hoop for my second point.'

*I never meant to hurt or upset you.*
*But Joshua, you have to realize it isn't healthy*
*to let this negativity build up inside.*
*Sometimes you just have to say enough*
*and believe in the person you've become.*

'He smacks the ball from my hand, dribbles the ball between his legs, then sinks the corner three.'

But what if who I am is the problem?
Maybe I'm just a fundamentally broken person.

'I trip over my legs as I go for the layup. The ball goes careening off the backboard.'

And I can say it was the way I grew up.
Blame the Oklahoma wind.
Blame the hollow walls of church halls.
But I keep ending up right back here.
That's who I am. I don't know any other way.

*You can say that as much you want,*
*but that's not the Joshua I know.*
*You can create conflict for yourself as much as you want,*
*keep chasing a plot of your own demise,*
*but I've heard your laugh more lately.*

'We exchange a few shots. He makes it look easy. I give everything just for a few lucky bounces.'

I have made some great memories
in recent days, haven't I.
Why couldn't they have lasted a little longer?
Surrounded by people who loved me, the real me.
But everyone keeps graduating and moving away.
Even Jenna and I aren't talking anymore.
For a moment, I had the world.
Why did it have to slip away?

'I grab the rebound, only to have the ball slip through my fingers and roll out of bounds.'

*That's life, I'm afraid.*
*The highs, the lows.*
*But you're still you.*

That's the problem. Who even is that?
My faith isn't as strong as they may think.
I'm not a good singer. Not a great talker.
Can't even win in the ring anymore.
Look at me! A short, little, oddly dressed boy.
I'm not man enough.
I'm definitely not feminine enough.
Why can't I just figure this out?

*Because you're human!*
*You're trying to be a character in a story.*
*Imagining yourself the way you think they see you.*
*All those uncertainties, that's what makes you, well you.*
*Just be yourself. I promise you, the rest will write itself.*

'He knocks another shot in; he has a commanding lead at this point. He passes me the ball. I hold it in my hands. Look up at the hoop.'

You're right. I know that.
I'm still trying to accept it.
Some days it's hard to, but thanks to you,
I'm learning to live with, not for this story.
And when I do, I really do feel happy.
Happy with where I'm at. Happy with who I am.

'I drill it from behind the arc. I look back at him. His breath is beginning to run short. I watch the sweat drop from his face.'

Hey Soj, are you okay?
You're always there for me.
You look out for me; you keep me in check.
You're the best kind of friend I could imagine.
You deserve to live your own story as much as me.
Don't think you have to stay on the side forever.
You're more than just a feeling.
I see it in your eyes, the hopes and dreams.
Every you've word said to me,
I think you're just waiting for someone to say to you.
Soj, go, figure out who you are.
You've given me that much; I want to give you the same.
It's okay. I'll be okay.

'He takes the ball one more time. Dribbles a few times, his footwork is always one step ahead of mine. He takes the shot. Nothing but net. Final score: 21-13, him. He's always been the better athlete. We begin walking off the court, talking, laughing like two old friends.'

*Hey Joshua...*
*...thank you.*

# You're More Than

You're more than the world will say you are.
You're pretty, you're kind,
but you also have such a creative mind.
That's worth something if you ask me.
You're more than your wins.
You're more than your insecurities.
You're more than your worst days.
So, remember that on the day
you get back a bad grade on a test.
Never let your self-worth be tied
to a number on a piece of paper.

People will tell you one thing
then expect the opposite from you.
They'll praise you. They'll tear you down.
And I know how hard it all is to understand.
There will be days where it feels
like all your friends hate you.
But I'll still love you. I hope you know that.

You're more than the world will say you are.
You're pretty, you're kind,
but you're also a complete mess.
And I love you for that.
You're more than your wins.
You're more than your insecurities.
You're more than your worst days.
So, remember that on the day
that boy breaks your heart.
I know you love him,
but you deserve to love yourself too.

Some say my life advice is ill-advised. Damn right.
It's okay to punch bullies. Kick their teeth in.
It's okay to fall in love a few times.
It's okay to fall down,
but you better pick yourself up again.
It's okay to make mistakes.
That's how you know you're still alive.
It's okay to follow your dreams.
And it's okay to choose new ones.

You're more than. You're more than.
The expectations. The ratings.
You're more than. You're more than.
The obligations. The beauty.
You're more than. You're more than.

You're more than the world will say you are.
You're pretty, you're kind,
but you're also such a badass kid.
I know that may be a bad word, but it's true.
You're more than your wins.
You're more than your insecurities.
You're more than your worst days.
So, remember that on the day
you get into a fight with your parents.
They love you, but they're
still human just like us.

Don't ever forget who you are;
my sister, I'll always love you.
And remember, I'd do anything for you.

# What She Was Told

And she said she never learned.
She said she never cared about herself.
Was taught to put others first and herself last.
It's what we heard as kids,
and it stuck with us like a virus in our conscience.
Love others and stop loving yourself.

What she was told–I heard it growing up too–
is to be kind, to be loving,
to smile every day for the sake of everyone else.
What she was told, the only way to be happy
is to be sure everyone else is laughing.
What she was told, looking out for yourself is selfish.
That the world would be a better place
if we only could set aside our pride.
And yet, now we don't know how to love ourselves.

We live in a world of undefined priorities,
where we have everything and nothing at once.
Love in the following order: God, family, friends.
Care for the orphans, watch out for the widows.
None of that's wrong. Love others, heal the world.
But how far does she have to drop in priority
before she can tend to herself?
When you give everything, you're left with nothing.
And if this love dissipates, she'll suffocate.
My dear, it's okay to love yourself.

Who is there for her when she hides from the world,
hoping no one sees her tears?
This feeling isn't absent, just out of sight.
She hides love so deep inside,
only show it to those on the outside.

Every second caring for another,
never knowing how to care for herself.
My dear, it's okay to love yourself.

What she was told–I heard it growing up too–
is to be kind, to be loving,
to smile every day for the sake of everyone else.
What she was told, the only way to be happy
is to be sure everyone else is laughing.
What she was told, looking out for yourself is selfish.
That the world would be a better place
if we only could only set aside our pride.
And yet, now we don't know how to love ourselves.

She let herself drift away, like dust in the wind.
These tears won't go away,
they're a part of who we are,
what we grew up thinking was the only way.
Every day I try so desperately
to show others I love them.
Because if I can give another a reason to smile,
I won't have to deal with the fact I hate my own.
These tears are just who we are.
Read these words, hear this song,
please know heartbreak isn't the only way.
Don't you see? See the pain living in her eyes?
She's trying so hard.
You can't save the world,
if you can't save your own heart.
You can't fill the world with love,
if you can't find love in yourself.
My dear, it's okay to love yourself.

My dear, no matter what you were told,
it's okay to love yourself.

# Unwilling Growth

I didn't mean to learn my lesson.
I wasn't trying to be more mature,
that happened by accident.
I don't want to grow and change,
but it keeps happening anyway.

The theme of the week has been self-respect.
I thought I got rid of mine,
but I accidently found it again.
Turns out I do have a limit; finally crossed that line.
Realized I deserve better than nothing at all.

So sick of the two-faced mean girl persona.
Seduce and sedate me, leave me in a coma.
Said cognitive dissonance is sexy.
I'll dance with my worst insecurities.
Dodge a bullet while holding a magnet.
There may be kindness in those eyes,
but the shit talking says otherwise.
Don't need all these pretend friends
who lie every time they say they care.
In my head there's someone who does,
took me listening to myself to remember so.

The older I get, the messier my résumé is.
I can't unwrite the words sitting on your bookshelf.
They were true then, don't know if they're true now.
But they were my story,
I'm learning to be okay with that.
We all grow up with time, don't we?

Chased validation with no intention in mind.
Told myself it'd be easier to accept my faults
if I never let go of my self-hating thoughts.
I would try and fail to get drunk,
leave the bar sober and pissed.
Saying I'm going to get better
just so I can get worse again.

And for all that frustration, the world doesn't
look as black and white anymore.
When did my politics go from
radical to reasonable?
I don't want common sense,
I want to be a punk reactionary.
But anger doesn't get you anywhere.
Downplaying violence is how you get shot.
And ranting to the reflection on a phone screen
doesn't make our community any safer.
Change is made with tired hands.

Now on to the list of things I'm never going to do again.
Heartbroken, said I'd never fall in love.
Hungover, said I'd never drink again.
Head aching, said I'd never pick up my gloves.
Won't fall for it, won't let myself get hurt,
until I do all three again next Thursday.

I really do want to be a better person.
Been trying to stop swearing so much.
Discovered it's easier to make friends with a hello.
Don't write someone off before the story starts.
They say confidence is attractive, but maybe
confidence is just knowing you're worth something.
And I didn't mean to,
but I think I've finally realized that.

# Makeup Bag

Jenna, you bitch. I miss you.
You left just as I was getting to know you.
Why did you have to go?
Just give me a reason.
Where did the wind take you to?
You were gone with the season.
When they ask about you, I say you're not real.
But you were real to me.

A makeup bag collecting dust.
You're the ghost haunting my dreams.
My love forever changed.
You're the girl haunting these pages.
A story stuck in perpetuity.

I was clearing out my closet the other day
and I found one of your shirts left behind.
It's a shame, I learned to write in your name
right before we stopped talking.
Got your signature in my journal,
and you got me to blame for your heartache.
Why did you have to go?
I've been saying this whole time you left me,
but let's be honest, I'm the one who left you behind.

I watched as you did up your makeup,
all while talking about loving who you are.
You helped me learn how to not hate my face,
taught me what it means to have grace.
And then I went and made friends that way,
I stopped pretending to be confident and just was.
Don't think I could have done it without you
showing me there's another way to live life.
A better way. A happier way.

A makeup bag collecting dust.
You're the ghost haunting my dreams.
My love forever changed.
You're the girl haunting these pages.
A story stuck in perpetuity.

I admire you for being undeniably yourself.
Spending your weekends gay and happy.
You're patient and still the rest of the week.
You're pretty and you know it.
In touch with your emotions.
You pray more than me.
You sing like it means something.
But most of all, you love your name
and everything that comes with it.
And y'know, I think I can finally say the same.

chapter viii

# finding purpose in the mundane parts of life

there was no big moment or declaration.
life doesn't make sense all at once.
if i want to be a good person—i do—
then it will be the million small things
that get me through.
if i want to smile again—i will—
then it will be a daily choice to do so.
every mountain has its peak,
every show has its climax,
but some of the best moments will be had
during the plateau and hiatus.

# A Quiet World

There was a blip in time when the world was quiet.
Everything seemed so simple,
we could remember what mattered.
Life and death, love and fear, my dear, when did we let it go?

Remember when the world was quiet?
Sixteen and in love, scared but braver than ever.
Learning to drive when there was nowhere to go.
Sitting at home, anxious all the time, trying to be strong
for those you love, praying for their safety every night.
In dark times we held a peace only found in the soul and mind.

Remember when the world was quiet?
A smile on a screen meant the world.
We were overjoyed just to hear the sound of a friend's voice.
And all this in a time when many died as a sacrifice,
away from the love they had always known.
In death, we were finally grateful to be alive.
On our knees praying for people we never knew.
Put our hope in the heroes risking their lives to save who we love.
Why did it take the world breaking apart
to bring us together again?

In a world of terror we found peace,
a quiet inside of each of us.
We learned to get by with love
and found trust in the unknowable.
In the midst of all the screaming we had a moment of silence.
When did we let it go?
There was a blip in time when the world was quiet.
Everything seemed so simple,
we could remember what mattered.
Life and death, love and fear, my dear, when did we let it go?

Remember when the world was quiet?
At once everything was different,
we were scared, we were careful.
Things changed, was it for the better?
In a time of death and disease, all was still.
People were screaming, but the streets were calm.
The parks belonged to the birds again.
The row of offices became a ghost town.
For once, our homes were places to live,
not just a place to keep our stuff.

When the world began to heal we just got sicker.
Twisted and even wickeder.
The peace scared us, the silence startled us,
so we returned to the white noise of panic
to drown out the sounds from our mind.
Why does it seem we grew accustomed to pain,
learned to keep screaming instead of keep praying?
It took the world ending for us to stop yelling,
but it wasn't long before we just got louder.
We let the plague take hold of us.
Left the quiet world behind.
It was life and death, we knew what was truly important,
but now all we know is death.

In a world of terror we found peace,
a quiet inside of each of us.
We learned to get by with love
and found trust in the unknowable.
In the midst of all the screaming we had a moment of silence.
When did we let it go?
There was a blip in time when my world was quiet.
Everything seemed so simple,
I knew what mattered the most.
Life and death, love and fear, my dear, how do I go back there?

# One Drink

After one drink it looked like I had died.
After two glasses of wine I sat there and cried.

Been writing this book for a while now.
Really ever since I finished that purple one.
I was desperate for a way to say what I shouldn't.
To understand something I couldn't.

After three drinks the pain and joy both felt numb.
After four shots of something else I just felt dumb.

After five drinks I prayed I would stop caring.
After six bitter ales I began needless swearing.

I wanted everyone to think it hadn't got to me.
It had. Took admitting that for it to stop hurting.
The more I wrote about it, the more it felt like a memory.
I started to see my story a little differently than before.

After seven drinks I felt fine.
After eight empty bottles I started to get on with my life.

After nine drinks my smile felt real again.
After ten mixed cocktails the healing could begin.

What once was all I could write about
was now just a chapter in who I was and who I am.
I was happy. I was content. It took months,
took some hard days for me to say it was a good year.

After eleven drinks I forgot what I was writing about.
And after twelve, I no longer felt the need to count.

# Back to the Basics

Wake up. Get out of bed. Take the first step.
Make sure I eat a full meal.
It's the simple things I tend to overcomplicate.
Shower. Get dressed. Smile around friends.
Don't forget to breathe.

I'm going back to the basics.
Learning to jab before I cross.
Learning to breathe before I talk.
I'm going back to the basics.
Remembering to step as I weave.
Remembering to be nice to the people I meet.

As a kid I thought my parents had it all figured out.
And now these kids think I'm the best fighter in town.
All I know how to do is take one hit too many.
What idiot thinks at twenty they got it all solved?
It's naïve really. What ever made me think that?

Put too much stress on these bones.
Learned they'll snap before they bend.
Now even the simple things are exhausting.

I'm going back to the basics.
Learning to jab before I cross.
Learning to breathe before I talk.
I'm going back to the basics.
Remembering to step as I weave.
Remembering to be nice to the people I meet.

# Driving in the Sky

We're driving in the sky!
Life is our apple pie!
The last and only two spies
who can avoid all the lies we cry.

Feel the air comin' from the road?
That's what today is about, bro.
Nothing's the same when there's no more rain.
No more rain to cause a world of pain.
Popsicle sticks and ice cream,
it's the same feeling.
You and I, we're playing Mario Kart,
I'll show you a trick and then dart,
right past the old restaurants and Walmart.

We're driving in the sky!
Life is our apple pie!
We're driving in the sky!
Life is our apple pie!

This Sunday my friend,
we're coming to summer's end.
So, until we get to be brothers again,
don't forget to write a song about
how we're driving in the sky.
Oh, we're driving in the sky!
Life is our apple pie!

How's school this year?
Across the street, see those trees,
near the park we played on as kids.
Who am I kidding, you still got all that ahead of you.
You have your friends, even when summer ends,
you'll prove 'em all again.
Every night for the past who-knows-how-many years
I'd walk by your door after you fall asleep,
wish you a goodnight and say I love you.

We're driving in the sky!
Life is our apple pie!
We're driving in the sky!
Life is our apple pie!

Hey kid, you'll always be my brother,
life is a search for what we discover.
You're such a cool person,
artistic and creative, kind and smart.
Even if I'm not in the room next to yours
we'll still be driving in the sky.
We're driving in the sky!
Life is our apple pie!

# Schoolbus

Before I met Soj, I had my fair share of friends in my head.
Nowadays they call me crazy,
back then I was just a kid with an imagination.
Playing with stuffed animals on my bedroom floor,
my sister and I creating characters out of thin air.
Before I met Soj, I had Samantha to argue with,
only to turn around and be best friends again.
We'd fight then make things right,
not because we were sorry, just bored.

All the stories in my head mean nothing
without someone to tell them to.
Got these friends in my head,
but I can only talk to them so much
before I need someone by my side instead.

Been creating tales and fantasies
while I walk since I was little.
Told them to my sister whenever she'd listen.
Before I met Soj, it was Sam who was the
sounding board for all my worst ideas.
She and I still talk each week,
and I'm still out there telling stories on my walks.
Writing them down in my notes app,
turning those notes into songs for this book,
a book I plan to share with all my friends.
Because all the stories in my head mean nothing
without someone to tell them to.

# Your Accomplishments

Some of my best memories are of other people's lives,
watching you and your accomplishments.
What would any of us be without the others?
All those years stuck under the same roof.
We would play with toys on our bedroom floor,
now I get to watch you hold a diploma.
We would kick a ball around the living room,
now I see you take the stage in front of everyone.

Eh, sure we use to fight.
And sure, we still do sometimes.
Though for every ten reasons I could give for why
you two are the worst sister and brother imaginable,
I could probably find a hundred that contradict it.
Stayed together even when things fell apart.
And we still regularly get together to tell stories
and sing songs just like when we were younger.

I've had my share of great moments,
and you two were there for me on those days.
Now you're getting older too.
You don't need me to drive you to school anymore.
Instead, we meet up to go to work events together.
You're not always going to need me to write for you.
Instead, I watch you hit each note all on your own.
So, when you think back on your accomplishments,
revisit the memories of the days you took the stage,
just know I was in the crowd
cheering you on the whole time.

# I'll Die a Stubborn Bastard

I don't quit, even when I should.
I'll keep lifting till the bar drops.
I'll keep fighting till I collapse on the mat.
I'm overly cautious till I have something to prove.

My resilience is a result of stupidity.
Won't check the mask before I put it on.
Won't think of alternatives before I'm done.
Watch me freeze in real time and say I'm fine.
Watch me not eat a thing and say I'll survive.

There's only one way down this mountain
and I'm going in blind.
There's only one way to end this fight
and I was never the betting favorite.
Too stubborn for my own good.
And I hate it when things work out my way.
I'm afraid I'll never learn.
If I gave up after I hit the snow I would have froze.
If I threw up after the first punch I would be broke.
But I didn't quit then, won't quit now,
for better or worse, I've survived.
Claim to be afraid of everything,
yet nothing has stopped me so far.
Say I won't just to prove myself wrong.
Living life with headstrong bravery.
Cry during the fight, take the win anyway.

My resilience is a result of stupidity.
Won't check the mask before I put it on.
I'd rather die than say I was never alive.

# Reunion

"Silvia, it's you!"
I run over and hug my friend.
It's a long one, neither of us want to let go.
"It's so good to see you again."
*It's good to see you, Joshua.*
I feel my eyes watering up.
"I'm sorry. I think about you all the time,
I really should have reached out sooner."
She smiles and tells me not to worry.
"I wish I had been a better friend.
I wish I could've been there when you needed me."
*But you're here now, aren't you?*
*Who cares about yesterday anyway.*
We talk for a while. I can't really tell about what.
The whole conversation feels like a blur.
But I know I'm happy.
"What are you writing these days?"
*I'm working on the third book in my series.*
*My agent is hoping we can release it by Christmas.*
*What about you? What book are you working on?*
I freeze. I always hate that question.
I'm not a real writer like her.
"It's just this silly little poetry collection,
I doubt anyone will ever read it."
*Well, I will. Just send me a copy when you're done.*
She smiles again. I hear music playing.

I sit up and rub my head.
Crawl out of bed and turn off my alarm.
I look back at my pillow and take a deep sigh.
"Silvia, I miss you."

# I Love You (Pt 1)

My mom held my hand before I could walk.
My dad read to me before I knew how to talk.
I've wasted more time sitting on the floor
with my sister than I have anyone else.
I've traded more inside jokes and laughter
with my brother than I could probably count.

Been meaning to write this song for a while now.
It's obvious to me,
but that doesn't mean I shouldn't say it aloud.
I love you. Always have, always will.

Remember August 24th?
Exploring the streets of Wichita.
On October 30th we had Coffee in Austin.
Playing games by the Pacific Ocean on October 25th.
You couldn't put a price on the memories I have with you,
you're the people who made me who I am.
And I love you.

Been meaning to write this song for a while now.
It's obvious to me,
but that doesn't mean I shouldn't say it aloud.
I love you. Always have, always will.

# Quietly Falling

I'm quietly falling in love.
Falling in love with life,
the beauty of art, the majesty of earth,
falling in love with you, in thought at least.
I'm quietly falling in love,
oh, quietly wondering.
Wondering why the world is such a show;
we show others we're in love,
can I show myself I'm in love?
I'm quietly alone, and that's okay.
I'm drinking my coffee,
calmed by all the books in the library.
I'm not on the party scene or social media,
instead I'm teaching myself to breathe,
so when I'm around friends I don't panic.
I'm quietly falling in love.
Falling in love with life,
the beauty of art, the majesty of earth,
I stand up just to fall in love with you again.
I want to fall... I want to shout...
I want to know what love is about.
I'm quietly falling in love.

# Healthy Living

Been trying to live better,
keep myself healthy.
Both mentally and physically.
Keep up spiritually and socially.
It's overwhelming,
but I'm still going to keep trying.

All I need in the morning is God and coffee,
and without either, the painkillers on my shelf,
but I've been trying to kick that habit.
Been trying to get out more,
to ignore the fact my apartment is a mess.

Ate a full meal today.
Got up early to work out.
There's still a pain in my stomach,
but hey, I finally booked that doctor's appointment.

All I need in the afternoon is paper and a pen,
and my playlist of sad music that I can't write without,
though some days I wouldn't mind if I could.
Been trying to finish this book,
to understand myself better than I did before.

Wrote in my prayer journal today.
Made someone laugh by being kind.
I don't drink every day,
but I think about her on all the ones that end in a why.

All I need in the evening is a prayer and a friend,
and occasionally a beer in hand,
that said I'm just as happy without one.
Been trying to be a better person,
to finally admit that's the best that I can do.

Been trying to live better,
keep myself healthy.
And I won't lie, it's been hard.
I still would say it's been worth it.
For all my obsessions and disassociation,
the countless wonder and stories I tell,
I want to live a healthy life.
I'm done with feeling sick all the time,
admitting that was the first step towards change.

All I need is a reason and the determination
to take care of this person I've begun to learn to love.

# Trust

When my words aren't enough.
On the days I can't control the world.
When a mess of thoughts is too much.
And I'm not sure what comes next.
You learn to trust.

The waves crashing. The boat shaking.
My Lord, your sky is crumbling down.
I let go of the bow. Grab hold of the wind.
My love, your heart will break in two.
The water rushing. The tide turning.
My, my, let the current guide us there.

When I don't know what to say.
On the days when I just don't understand.
When I need a different set of words.
And the path ahead is clouded in mystery.
You learn to trust.

# Knife

Nine o'clock at night. Walking south.
That man is following me again.
He lurks right in my shadow.
I know what he wants, the thug.
His harassment is the one constant.

I pull the knife from my pocket,
tap it against my right thigh.
And I hear him say, "Little boy walking all by himself."
"You really think you can escape?"
"I'd be careful in this part of town."
"The world can be a dangerous place."
"Especially for someone all alone."

Storm clouds in the sky. The terror in your eye.
I spin my blade, grip the handle tight.
He won't leave me alone.
I wipe my tears, time to say goodnight.

I'll do it. I'll cut you. Slit your throat.
Watch your blood pour into these storm drains.
And I hear him say, "Why are you so angry all the time?"
"You really think I want to hurt you?"
"I'd be careful with that attitude of yours."
"Don't let your emotions get the better of you."
"Especially for someone all alone."

My hands are trembling as I ready myself.
This has been long overdue. It's time to kill him once and fo-

I hear people talking up ahead.
It's my friends, they're across the block from me.
We embrace one another under the streetlamp.
My shadow runs away under the light.
I discreetly put the knife back in my pocket.
Don't see any need for it now.
But mark my word, sir,
you can't hide in that fog much longer.

## chapter ix

# a photo album full of random adventures

we didn't plan any of this.
you said you were bored,
i said i'm free after work.
been living vicariously through my stories
for two decades now.
letting my imagination guide my life.
for the first time i have actual stories to tell.
there's no need to change the names.
for some of my stories are imaginary,
but my friends, the photos with you are real,
and i won't forget a moment of them.

# Gas Station Latte

Gas station lattes and bathroom cocktails.
Something or another to get my heart going
cause I've been on little sleep these days.
Too busy staying up late as of late.
Meet my newest addictions and vices.
The adventures of my friends and I.
The stories I'm writing at every chance.

It's almost Christmas time again.
Where did the year go?
A mess of memories left in my head,
some good, a few bad, but they were all important to me.
Been recording the memories in my notes app,
writing about the lessons I learned.

All I want this year is to be in love again.
To cling to the smell of cheap perfume,
gasoline, and three dollar coffee.
I want to write like my life is on the line,
sleep deprived and desperate for time.

Peppermint mocha and homemade eggnog.
Some coffee and alcohol to keep my attention,
cause that's hard around this time of year.
Too busy staying up late as of late.
Meet my newest addictions and vices.
The adventures of my friends and I.
The stories I'm writing at every chance.

It's almost Christmas time again.
Where did the year go?
All I want is to be hopelessly enamoured again,
even if that ends me up in the middle of nowhere.
Been plotting the pieces to this year's gifts,
a way for me to say I love this.

Been feeling nostalgic for restless nights.
Evenings spent gazing into your eyes,
making friends in the cold wintertime.
Waking up before my alarm the next day
to write stories and love songs at 7am.

Gas station lattes and bathroom cocktails.
Something or another to get my heart going.
Gas station lattes and bathroom cocktails.
Here I am, another book in hand.
Here I am, with the best people I know.
Got a buzz before ever taking a sip.
Gas stations lattes and bathroom cocktails.
Something or another like that.

# Rendezvous

I remember the day and time.
Don't plan on forgetting it any time soon.
Got a picture saved to my phone.
It's not the best one, but it's got you all in it.
And now the photo is hanging on my fridge.
It is one of my favorite stories,
on one of my favorite nights.
And I won't forget it anytime soon.

We'll rendezvous by the fountain.
Walk the streets together again, my friends.
I love each one of you, did I say that yet?
It's possible I hadn't realized back then.

I know how stubborn I can be,
but man, if you told me to follow you, I would.
To the end of the earth,
I'd jump over the edge if you went first.

Tell her I miss her
and the random things she always says.
I tend to overthink just about everything,
but I think you had it right from the beginning.

We'll rendezvous by the fountain.
Walk the streets together again, my friends.
I love each one of you, did I say that yet?
It's possible I hadn't realized back then.

I trust you two like a brother and sister.
We'll spend the next year only growing closer.
And we'll find ourselves here again soon,
three unlikely friends lifting a glass together.

We stood side-by-side the whole time.
Laughed enough the smile on my face froze.
Made a few stupid decisions along the way,
I can't imagine regretting a single one.
The videos will live in infamy,
they may be grainy, the pictures a little blurry,
but the memories are still clear in my head.

We'll rendezvous by the fountain.
Walk the streets together again, my friends.
I love each one of you, did I say that yet?
And I have ever since that night.

Gave me a coin, I held it in my palm.
Watched each of them throw their coins in.
I gave one last prayer, tossed mine in,
and wished for this story to never end.

# Returned Call

I wasn't offended when you didn't pick up.
I knew you were probably busy.
But you called back a few minutes later.
Did I have a reason for calling? Not particularly.
I just needed to talk with someone.
You see, I wasn't having a great night.
Don't know if you could tell over the phone.
Did my thousand yard stare translate in tone?
We didn't talk long, but it was enough
that when I hung up I didn't feel so bad anymore.
It's hard to keep up the sad little emo boy act
when talking with you.

I've convinced myself before that it's okay to be friends
with people who barely tolerate you.
The kind of people who are always, "Too busy."
But despite when I give you a hard time,
you always manage to find some time for me.
We're not friends out of convenience,
and that's a nice change of pace if you ask me.

Call me anytime,
I meant it when I said I'll always be there.
If I don't pick up, just know I'll return your call.
You're my best friend, after all.
Don't feel like your problems
are an inconvenience to me.
And I know that's ironic for me to say,
but you've proven you'll always be there for me,
so there's no reason why I won't do the same.

# Sock

You don't judge me for falling flat on my face.
Which is one of my favorite pastimes.
You would just pick me up and give a hug.
I hope you know I'm always there when you need one.

Saying hello wasn't easy for me.
Saying goodbye was much worse.
You didn't see me cry. But I still did.
I was bragging about you only days after.
Telling everyone how great my friend is.
And I would be lying if I said I don't miss you.

I really want to be the smartest in the room,
but even more so I want to be in a room with friends.
What I'd give to just sit and listen to music,
spend hours on your living room floor,
cider and wine, board games and movies.
Kick off my shoes, lie on the carpet,
a pair of socks on my feet,
telling you all about the songs I'm writing,

Tend to make a lot of mistakes,
said some things I rather regret,
but I made the right choice to trust you.
Won't for a second rethink the decision to be your friend.
And I'll make it to you one of these days.
Hand this book to you myself.

# The First Two

Sat behind you for years.
Have pictures of us older than my memory.
You've been there my whole life,
but I missed the first month and three days of yours.
We bickered and talked our way through childhood,
but even growing up couldn't keep us apart.
It was back in the fifth grade,
we were always the first two in the room.

Grew up in Sunday school.
Listening and obeying every rule.
Passed notes during the sermon.
Told stories in the backseat.

There's been a few times you've
changed the way I think.
And I know I've made a difference to you
just by keeping around.
Being friends with you gives me
the confidence to be friends with anyone.

In our youth they would call us smart,
now I'd say we're nearly clueless
about near about everything.
And I don't think I'd want it any other way.
But even still, when we're together
there ain't a teacher, preacher, or idiot
that can outsmart us two.

Grew up in Sunday school.
Anymore they would call me a fool.
Now we meet for drinks just down the street.
Say cheers before the first two shots.

# Used to Be

Hadn't talked to you in roughly 540 days.
Wasn't sure if or when we would again.
But over the holiday break we got in touch,
after more than a year we finally met for lunch.

It used to be you and I, inseparable friends,
but times change and so do people.
I'm a different person than the kid you used to know.
And I like to think you're better
than the worst memories I have of you.

You're not my best friend anymore,
in a way that hurts to say.
It's okay, I still love you. You're still my friend,
and I'm happy we both get to live our own lives.
If this was bound to happen eventually,
at least we still talk here and there.

Things aren't the same,
but change isn't always for the worse.
I don't think either of us thought
we'd end up where we are.
But look at us both, living lives worth living.
I'm happy for you.
I hope life treats you well,
I could never wish anything but the best for you.

It used to be you and I, bestest of friends,
but times change and so do people.
I've grown so much these past few years.
And I like to think at the end of the day
if I asked you, the same would be said.

# I Miss You

The older I get,
the harder it becomes to go though my contacts list.
I could find six, at the very least,
people I promised to talk with again.
I think about them regularly.
I never text. I don't call.
We were good friends once upon a time,
but I'm sorry, I haven't been as good of a friend lately.

The easiest part of moving is carrying furniture,
it's what comes next that's tough.
And I once claimed I'd move heaven and earth for you,
but I haven't moved an inch since.

I miss you. Not every day,
but a quite a few of them.
The next drink is on me.
Tell me all about your stories.
Every little miniscule word.
I'll reminisce on the ones we had together.
Hold to the photographs,
write the stories down so they stay a part of me.
Because I miss you.

*Hey! How've you been? Let's talk soon.*

# Grappling Distance

Stuck in grappling distance.
Fighting for a clinch.
Afraid to be taken down.
If I let someone close I have to let my guard down.
And I'm scared that will make me weak.

I'm more of a runner than a fighter.
More of an idealist than a winner.
I don't need anyone else.
I'm a kicker. I want you to stay away.
Don't grab hold of me.

But when life punches you in the face,
and you find yourself lying on the ground,
who's going to help pick you up from the floor?
Who's going to let their guard down to give you a hug?

I'm stuck in grappling distance.
I want to elbow away, pull back to kicking range.
But sometimes you have to get close to someone,
be honest with them, trust them, even love them,
and let them hold you when you feel all alone.

# I Love You (Pt 2)

He could make me believe in the impossible, like myself.
There are few people I feel more at ease with than him.
She sometimes reminds me of myself,
a little quiet but always has a smile.
Conversations with him never fail to be entertaining,
one of the best people to talk nonsense with for hours.

Been meaning to write this song for a while now.
It's obvious to me,
but that doesn't mean I shouldn't say it aloud.
I love you. So glad I've gotten to know you.

Remember January 9th?
Snow on the streets of Winter Park.
On December 19th we had dinner at my house.
Roasting s'mores by the fireside on October 18th.
Hardly a better way I could've have spent this evening,
around you all I get to be the best version of myself.
And I love you.

Been meaning to write this song for a while now.
It's obvious to me,
but that doesn't mean I shouldn't say it aloud.
I love you. So glad I've gotten to know you.

# Game Night

Sometimes when we're all sitting here,
a thought passes by in my mind.
I'm happy.
We're all laughing at our own jokes.
Or we're just talking about our lives.
No ulterior motives, no pressure or panic.
I don't feel the need to prove myself.
And I know in these moments there isn't
a place on this planet I rather be.
Simple as it could be.
I'm just happy.

# Real Friends

Driving alone in the snow,
I wanted to go on an adventure.
Stay up late, make mistakes, laugh the next day.
I've always believed I'll sleep when I'm dead.
Prayed for an exciting life around people I like,
I'd say what I got was even better.

Gambling at the poker table,
drinking in the basement.
We were all cramped and miserable,
but it's when you're at your worst
you realize who your real friends are.

After several years of toxic, negative people,
I had to re-teach myself what it meant to be a friend.
Constant cynicism doesn't make anyone happy.
And thanks to you, I remembered what it feels like
to not be an inconvenience all the time.
Proved to me it's possible to be confident in who you are
and I've been feeling more like myself ever since.

Gambling at the poker table,
drinking in the basement.
We were all cramped and miserable,
but it's when you're at your worst
you realize who your real friends are.

When I think back on the hours we wasted together,
I know there isn't a place I'd rather have been.
Driving around town in your car,
trying to fit the five or six of us in two seats to few.
Some days my accomplishments seem silly to me,
but you each are happy to see me succeed.
So just you know, I've got your back till the very end.

You invited me to lunch, I offered to drive.
Showed up at my house randomly
in the middle of an ice storm.
And that was stupid, but at this point I've lost count
of all the stupid things we do when we're together.
Jumping off roofs, lifting heavy machinery, losing sleep,
trying to induce frostbite, rolling down snowy hills.

Think of all the crazy stories we'll tell for years to come.
The nights playing games at my kitchen table.
Eating and drinking in one another's company.
The world never felt more free.
Together we're at our best,
and that's when you realize who your real friends are.

Some nights I'll blink,
wondering if I've imagined all this.
But here we are, sitting around a campfire,
talking about life.
And there are few feelings more real than that.

chapter x

# the calming nature of fidgeting with a necklace

got a new place, moved all my books last week.
placed my jewelry on the dresser.
the flimsy cardboard boxes that
hold my life in them.
every last adventure, each story told.
i walk back down university,
the dreams all returning to me.
the sun begins to fall below the tree line.
i hold the pendant of my necklace to my chest.
and somehow, life is always more beautiful
than any words i've found to say so.

# Ego Death

Another bruise. Another evening.
Though I'm not done yet.
Don't tell my friends.
I need to be the one to put this to an end.

I walk down a dark alleyway.
The shrewd streetlamps all that give light.
A crowd has gathered on both sides.
I strap my punching gloves,
spit my gum onto the concrete.
A man stands tall in my way.
Hello, my friend.
"You just couldn't live without me, could you?"
"How many scars do I have to leave before you learn?"
"Joshua, what business brought you back here?"

My business, you ask?
I'm the toy you pay only to break.
I'm the one who cleans blood with teeth.
I hear the cheers while my ears ring.
I'm the one who makes the sick sing.
You smile at the pain of my sin.
So, I'll tell you of my business:
I'm the one about to motherfucking win.

The fight starts like any other between us two.
He knocks me down. Throws me around.
But I just keep getting back up.
Every time I do my confidence just grows.
Hey, looks like I've gotten better, right?
In fact, I go as far to start taunting him.
Hey, how about you shut up and fight.
And I can see it getting to his head.

"You're an emotional little kid who needs to grow up!"
He's shaking in his stance, spit flying as he speaks.
"Stop letting these stupid fucking feelings control you!"
He throws a jab, I calmly slip to the side.

We dance around each other for a moment.
The angrier he gets, the more fear I see in those eyes.
His guard beginning to slip.
I switch my stance back, throw my right leg to his head.
The kick lands. And so do my next few punches.
He's taken aback. Hey, Cloudy Eye!
Looks like I got more fight in me than you thought.

"Kid, you better shut your mouth
if you know what's good for you!"
He responds with a swift round kick to the leg.
A distinct snapping sound echoes around.
I fall to the ground, wreathing in pain.
I lie there, clutching my leg,
tears streaming down my face.

"Where are your friends at now?"
"They don't care about you, you realize that!"
"I told you that punk Soj was just a coward."
"If he really loved you, he'd be here, right?"
"And where's that queer little freak, Jenna at?"
"She's gone. You ran her off. Just like you always do."
"You're the reason everyone
who tries to love you leaves!"

I close my eyes. The voice of Soj ringing in my head.
*Get up.* I see my parents smiling at me.
*Get up.* I hear my students celebrating to the side.
*Get up.* My friends and I falling in the snow.
*Get up.* One of them reaches their hand out to help me.
I get my feet under me and stand back up.
My leg is shaking, barely holding my weight.
But remember, I always stand again.

"What are you doing?!"
"You will never win this fight!"
He swings his arm back. I shoot in and grab hold.
We wrestle. I can feel him struggling.
Finally, I get my arm around his throat,
hold him in a rear choke.
Just tap, I tell him. It's over, don't hurt yourself.
He won't, so I prepare for what must come next.

"You think you're all that.
You're a failure, you hear me!"
"Stop letting the world tell you otherwise!"
"You need me! You can't live without me!"
"I'm your only real frie-"
I snap my arms across his neck.
When I release my grip, he falls to the floor.
His eyes blacken. The clouds inside evaporate.
I stand above him, still shaking.
The lights immediately start to dim.
The crowd fades away as if they
never existed to begin with.
I drop to my knees.
Goodbye, my friend.

# Proud of Myself

This poem will never make it to publication,
but I wanted to say I'm proud of myself.
For all the hours spent writing about my fears,
I don't feel so fearful anymore.
And for all the time I wasted on anger with myself,
I've found a reason to be kind instead.
I'm becoming the person I told people I would be.
Not so scared of putting myself out there.
Not so irritated by the life in front of me.
And even when everything inside of me hurts,
I know I'm still out here trying my best.
And happily so.
I'm proud of myself for that.

# Profile Picture

You updated your profile photo recently.
I stared at that button-sized picture of you
longer than I care to admit.
Just a small glimpse of your life these days.
I used to be able to ask you how've you been,
anymore this is the only way to keep in touch.
And while I miss seeing your face,
I miss hearing your voice far more.
I've got more than not,
but I'd give a lot just to talk.
To catch up with you and clear the air,
hear about how your life has been.
I've been happy lately, I just want you to know.
I wish you nothing but the same.

# Promises

School starts again next week.
I promise this isn't another poem about... *oh, forget it.*
I've been thinking again, never really stopped.
About you, about my friends, about everything really.
I made a few promises recently.
And this year I'm going to follow through.

Soj, I promised you I wasn't depressed.
Jenna, I promised to keep you close.
I don't know how well I hold to those words.
You both know me and my tells too well.

I blacked out another promise I made.
Been trying to keep it,
trying to forget the name.
I'll black you out of my memory.
A promise broken every time I write.
I know my word is only good as these words.

I made a promise during the last week of school.
To greet every person I meet with a smile.
To be a good friend. Knowing what that means.
To love people regardless of the past.
And I've broken promises before.
I'm going to keep this one.

James, I promise you,
I'll speak up and speak my mind.
Kaleigh, I promise you,
I won't ever speak ill of any of you.
I vow to be better than my worst instincts.

Payton, I promise you,
I'll become a better person each day.
Jake, I promise you,
this world will be a greater place cause of us.
I vow to prove what you all said about me right.

Isabella, I promise you,
I won't ever forget where I came from.
Tagen, I promise you,
I'll be friendly even on the days when it's hard.
I vow to remember the best in each of you.

Hold me to these words.
I promise I'm going to eat today.
I promise I won't say anything hateful in the mirror.
I promise to take care of myself.
I've been trying to not let myself down,
and I'm getting better, but it's still hard some days.
But I know for a fact I won't let you down.

# I Love You (Pt 3)

Been trying to convince other people to love me.
Hide my flaws, play up my quirks and strengths.
But I can't hide these thoughts from my own brain.
Been trying to convince others,
can I just convince myself that I'm worth something?
When I hear the words out loud it makes so much sense.

Been meaning to write this song for a while now.
It isn't always obvious to me,
but I'm still trying to say it aloud.
I love you. At my best, at my worst.

Remember last night?
Walking the streets of Norman again.
On November 4th I wrote a poem in the dark,
rain crashing against the window of a coffee shop.
These words couldn't have come at a better time,
because they were the words I needed to hear.
I love you. I mean it, I'm trying to at least.

Been meaning to write this song for a while now.
It isn't always obvious to me,
but I'm still trying to say it aloud.
I love you. At my best, at my worst.

# Let Go

I had this idea to write down all the things worrying me.
Get all this stress on paper and out of my head.
I would then look at the list and realize it wasn't that bad.
But I don't think I should follow through.
Because, y'know, I'm starting to think
the last thing I need is another list.

I'm learning, on my own,
the things school never could've taught me.
Learning to let go. Discovering how to live for myself.
Learning love means more than a feeling.
It's found in the way I live each day.

If I could get it through my head once and for all
that I'm more accomplished when I don't list my vices.
I get more done on the days in which
I don't sit around worrying about tomorrow.
You get farther by walking than pointing.

I'm learning, on my own,
the things school never could've taught me.
Learning to let go. Discovering how to live for myself.
Learning love means more than a feeling.
It's found in the way I live each day.

I'm learning, on my own,
it's easier to write when you let go.
Let go of those feelings of inadequacy and fear,
and instead listen to what's around you.
Smile and listen to your own laughter.

# Running Out of Time

I don't want to finish writing this book.
There's too many stories I still need to complete.
I'm not ready to say goodbye to this chapter of my life.
I don't want to miss the friends on the pages.

If I say goodnight
then how will I know the memories will live?
I don't want to say goodbye,
I don't want to close the page.
Been holding onto this journal for 3½ years now,
and now the pages are nearly full.
The binding is frayed, some pages falling from grace.
I've carried this with me for so long,
how can I just put it to rest?
Can't I just have one more moment of time?

I've been writing myself as a character.
Living just to further the plot.
I don't even call myself by my name,
but simply the writer of these thoughts.
This story is inseparable from who I am,
no amount of trying to distance myself from it
will change the words I scribbled on the paper.

All year I've been working tirelessly on this story.
Why does it feel like a part of me has to die
for this book to finally conclude?
This was my life, my stories, my friends,
for the better part of the past year it was all mine.
And if I had nothing else I'd still be happy.
As long as these words live, I'll be fine.

Running out of pages,
running low on time.
Trying to fill the spaces, edit all the lines.
Gave myself a deadline,
I think I smiled when I said it's time.
Bittersweet as any ending is.

So, as I rest my pen and close the page,
as I sit here and as I pray,
I will not let these words die on my shelf.
I will cherish them, hold to the memories fondly,
and finally be who I told people I'd be.
I will go out and make new stories,
poems and photos, memories and music,
share them with my friends and family,
and God willing, reach what's past me.
And I will always have you, my journal,
to return to for advice and nostalgia.

# Saying Goodbye (For Now Anyway)

Take another glance out that old window.
There in the backyard we grew up in.
All the friends I made over the years.
Some stayed and some went away.
They were real. They were in my mind.
They made me, well, me.
I'm older now, not a kid anymore,
and it's finally time to say goodbye.

To my imaginary girl, my Oklahoma girl,
your laugh still makes me smile.
You were strong. You were beautiful.
Don't force yourself into the shadows,
the world deserves to know you.
And even now that we go our different ways,
I'll always keep a part of you in my heart.

To the part of me I killed in self-defense,
I kneel at your grave.
Place a bouquet on the ground.
The clouds are clear in the sky.
If only you didn't have to die.
I think you were lonely; you hated yourself,
and you thought if you could make me live in fear
than you wouldn't have to be so alone.
My friend, I hope your soul finds peace.

To the one that grew up by my side,
I finally put your black diary away.
It's time to put our childhood to rest.
I pray that one day we may meet again.
I wouldn't be the man I am without
the years of friendship we shared.
Through heartache and pain, you and I stayed.
Dried your tears on my shoulder.
You may be a world away,
but you'll always have a place in my heart.

And to my imaginary best friend,
Soj, all I can say is thank you.
For everything.

To all of my imaginary friends,
it's time for me to grow up now.
I want to say goodbye. I need to thank you.
For all the good times we had,
for staying with me through the hard days.
Now I'll go and follow after those dreams we had.
I'm growing up,
I hope you're proud of me.

To all of my imaginary friends,
I love you.
Which in a roundabout way is me
finally saying that I love myself.

# Changing Seasons

I was sitting on the floor, across from Tagen.
Surrounded by cardboard boxes,
we were talking about everything on our minds.
It was an honest conversation,
the type I've learned to stop avoiding.
He had just started his new job,
I was in the middle of moving.
There was that feeling that things
were about to change again.
And this time around I felt ready.

I lifted a glass with Isabella on my 21st birthday.
More than two decades gone by and we're still friends.
As I wait on my next drink I start to think of
all the years of bittersweet memories.
We're not the same little kids who grew up
memorizing Bible verses together.
And yet, through every version of her and I
we managed to stay close friends.

An entire afternoon spent with Jake.
He was moving back home soon,
and man, you know I'll miss you.
As we sat there eating dinner together,
there was a feeling of change looming near.
But that isn't always a bad thing, right?
If people never grew or changed,
how would we go on to live such great lives?

I was hanging decorations with Abigail.
She really is all grown-up now,
and I'm nothing but proud to call her a friend.
I got to watch it firsthand,
see her become the amazing person she is.

There are moments where I decided to be different,
where I didn't let anxiety stop me from opening up.
Sitting in silence with Kaleigh and Rachel.
Sometimes nothing needs to be said, you just know.
There are some people who you just trust like that.
And I had never felt more at home with friends than
when Perry shouted my name across a tennis court.
She got a smile out of me when all I ever want to do is scowl.

I was standing on the sideline
coaching the kids who I've watched grow up.
They used to be so little, look at them now.
Fighting for themselves, winning more than I ever did.
And I hear them all talking and laughing,
the cheers they raise for each of their friends.

Payton and I racing down a mountain,
I never could beat her.
It shouldn't really be any secret that I look up to her.
She's the kind of friend I aspire every day to be.
I watch her hit the run out before me.
A few seconds later I come to a stop on her left side.
She asked if I want to run it back one more time
And I smiled, knew I'd be a little less afraid this round.

The long, late night drives with James,
in the middle of nowhere with nothing to talk about
so we talked about everything we could.
When we look back on these days
I think those are the memories we'll remember best.
All the countless small moments,
making jokes, learning life lessons, growing up.
These are the stories we're writing.

I was driving home the other night.
Took a look in my rearview mirror and smiled.

# Index

Paragon
Coalition

# CONTENT

## ACKNOWLEDGMENT

I would like to express my sincere gratitude to all the authors who have unknowingly provided endless inspiration for this humor book. Your quirks, idiosyncrasies, and funny ways have made the writing process a joyous adventure. To the authors who roam the streets muttering to themselves, thank you for reminding me that it's perfectly normal to have conversations with imaginary characters. Your passion for your craft is infectious.

I owe a debt of gratitude to the authors who have perfected the art of eavesdropping. Your ability to turn snippets of everyday conversations into hilarious dialogue has pushed me to sharpen my listening skills. A special thanks to the authors who carry their notebooks or voice recorders everywhere they go. Your dedication to capturing ideas, on the go, has reminded me of the importance of always being prepared for a stroke of brilliance.

To the authors who can get lost in their imagination, thank you for showing me the beauty of wandering off into fictional worlds. Your ability to zone out mid-conversation has permitted me to embrace my own moments of creative daydreaming. My appreciation goes out to all the authors who have mastered the art of procrastination. Your ability to find every possible distraction has taught me the importance of taking breaks and finding inspiration in unexpected places.

To the authors who engage in spirited arguments with their characters, thank you for reminding me that even fictional beings can challenge and surprise us. Your imaginary conversations have brought laughter and depth to my own writing. I extend my thanks to the authors who pace back and forth while deep in thought. Your restless energy has shown me the power of physical movement in stimulating creativity.

To the authors who find humor in the mundane, thank you for reminding me to always look for the funny side of life. Your ability to turn everyday situations into hilarious tales has added a touch of comedy to my writing. I am indebted to the authors who have shared their quirky writing rituals. Your unique superstitions and habits have reminded me that creativity often thrives in the realm of the unconventional. To the authors who possess the gift of witty comebacks and puns, thank you for reminding me that laughter can be found in the most unexpected places. Your sharp wit has inspired me to inject humor into my work.

I would like to express my appreciation to the authors who immerse themselves in extensive research. Your dedication to authenticity and humor has encouraged me to explore the bizarre and obscure. To the authors who have generously shared their hilarious anecdotes and stories from the writing journey, thank you for reminding me that even the most challenging moments can be transformed into comedic gold.

To the authors who embrace descriptive language in everyday conversations, thank you for showing me the power of turning mundane tasks into grand adventures. Your ability to add flair and humor to ordinary moments has inspired me. I am grateful to the authors who find solace in procrasti-baking. Your culinary creations have reminded me that creative outlets can take many forms.

Lastly, thank you to all the authors, both known and unknown, for your unintentional contributions to this humor book. Your hilarious ways have been a constant source of inspiration, and I am forever grateful.

Sincerely,
Irene Xanderena

# AUTHOR HUMOR

# INTRODUCTION

I started writing the humor series in 2023. Humans tend to approach life and their careers with great seriousness. But once they grasp the concept that life is akin to a game, they will find it more pleasurable.

Welcome to the wonderfully wacky world of authors! In this humor book, we'll embark on a hilarious journey through the quirks, eccentricities, and downright absurdities of the literary world. Authors of all shapes and sizes will take center stage as we dive into their peculiar habits, unusual rituals, and comical conversations with their characters. Authors, those imaginative beings who transport us to fantastical realms and captivate us with their words, often possess a delightful array of idiosyncrasies that make them as fascinating as the stories they create. Whether it's muttering to themselves in public, engaging in heated debates with their fictional creations, or pacing back and forth in search of inspiration, authors have a knack for infusing their lives with an extra dose of hilarity.

Authors have an uncanny ability to infuse laughter into their work, and throughout these pages, we will encounter the mischievous sense of humor authors possess. From the renowned literary giants to the unsung heroes of the writing realm, this book will celebrate the delightful quirks and comical antics that make authors a truly unique and entertaining bunch. Grab a cozy chair, and a cup of something warm, and get ready to embark on a side-splitting journey through the peculiar and humorous lives of authors. Buckle up, dear reader, Let the laughter begin!

# PREFACE

*"Laughter is like a good sneeze - it's contagious, slightly embarrassing, and leaves everyone wondering what the heck just happened."*
– Mark Twain [1835 – 1910]

Dear reader, Welcome to the humor series books! Together let's embark on the world of authors, where hilarity and imagination collide to create a literary landscape unlike any other. As you delve into the pages of this humor book, prepare yourself for the offbeat humor of brilliant puns. Why write a joke book about authors, you may ask? Well, the answer is simple: I'm one of them and we are a riot! From the classics to the contemporary, authors have a knack for infusing their lives with a delightful dose of humor, both intentional and unintentional. Our quirks and peculiarities make us fascinating creatures to observe and, let's be honest, laugh with.

This book isn't just a celebration of the authors themselves; it's also a tribute to the readers who find solace, joy, and laughter in their books. Throughout these pages, you'll encounter authors of all genres and eras. Together, we'll celebrate their wit, their creativity, and their ability to tickle our funny bones with their words. So, dear reader, it's time to put on your comedy glasses, open your heart to humor, and be transported to a place where laughter reigns supreme. As you turn the pages of this book, may it remind you of the joy that comes from the written word, and the magic that happens when authors embrace their innate sense of humor. And, above all, may it inspire you to appreciate the lighter side of literature and seek out the joyous moments within the stories we hold dear. I invite you to join me on this uproarious journey into the world of authors. Let's dive in and discover the laughter that lies within the pages. Happy reading!

Irene Xanderena

# AUTHOR HUMOR

**1**

Why did the author go to therapy?

They had too many "character" issues!

## 2

# What did the author say when their book got rejected?

"Guess I'll just have to "rewrite" my future!"

**3**

# Why did the author go broke?

Because they couldn't stop spending all their money on plot twists!

**4**

# Why did the author bring a ladder to the library?

Because they wanted to climb up the best-seller lists!

**5**

How do you make an author laugh?

Give them a "pun"-ctuation mark!

**6**

Why did the author become a baker?

Because they wanted to "whisk" their readers away to a different world!

# 7

## What did the book say to the author?

"I've got you covered, I'm a real page-turner!"

# 8

## Why did the author carry a notebook everywhere?

To jot down any "novel" ideas that popped up!

## 9

## Why did the author become a gardener?

They wanted to "plant" the seeds of creativity!

## 10

# Why did the author go to the therapist?

They had a serious case of writer's "block"!

# 11

## How do authors exercise their creativity?

## They do "book" squats and "novel" stretches!

## 12

# What did the author say after finishing their first book?

"That was a novel experience!"

## 13

Why did the author get kicked out of the library?

They were "checking out" too many puns!

## 14

What did the author say to their computer? "

You're my write-hand device!"

# 15

## What did the author say to their pencil?

"You're the 'write' tool for the job!"

## 16

# Why was the author always cold?

Because they had too many drafts!

## 17

Why did the author start a bakery?

Because they wanted to make some "dough" with their writing!

# 18

Why did the author bring a dictionary to the party?

Because they wanted to "define" the atmosphere!

## 19

# What's an author's favorite exercise?

Plot twists and turns!

## 20

# How do authors stay organized?

They use "plot" calendars!

## 21

What did the author say to their computer when it crashed?

"You've got some serious "plot" holes!"

## 22

# Why did the author become a chef?

Because they loved "cooking" up stories!

**23**

# What do you call an author who can juggle?

A "write"r of all trades!

## 24

## Why did the author bring a thesaurus to the interview?

To "synonym"ize their answers!

# 25

Authors have a way with words, but sometimes they can't find them when they're looking for their car keys.

## 26

# Authors are great at creating characters, but they often struggle with social interactions in real life.

## 27

# Authors can spend hours agonizing over the perfect sentence, only to delete it in the end.

# 28

Authors have a love-hate relationship with their own writing. One moment they think it's brilliant, the next they want to burn it all.

## 29

Authors have a knack for observing human behavior, which is why they make excellent people-watchers at coffee shops.

## 30

# Authors tend to eavesdrop on conversations, always on the lookout for interesting dialogue for their stories.

## 31

# Authors have a never-ending to-be-read pile that keeps growing faster than they can finish books.

## 32

# Authors can get lost in their own fictional worlds and forget to do basic things like eating or sleeping.

# 33

Authors have a collection of quirky writing rituals, like using a specific pen or wearing lucky socks.

# 34

Authors have a love for stationary that borders on obsession! Notebooks, pens, and colorful sticky notes are their best friends.

## 35

# Authors often have more conversations with their imaginary characters than with real people.

## 36

Authors have a habit of taking long walks or showers when they're stuck on a plot point, as if inspiration lies in the great outdoors or behind a shower curtain.

**37**

Authors can get emotionally attached to their fictional characters, sometimes even more than to real people.

## 38

# Authors have a love for procrastination, finding any excuse to avoid sitting down and actually writing.

## 39

# Authors have a talent for making up excuses when asked about their progress on a book.

# 40

Authors have a unique ability to turn everyday situations into potential plotlines, constantly thinking, "This would make a great story!"

## 41

# Authors tend to hoard books, always believing that they will need that one obscure reference someday.

## 42

Authors have a secret stash of half-finished manuscripts hidden away, waiting for the day when they muster the courage to revisit them.

# 43

Authors have a special bond with their fellow writers, understanding the struggles, joys, and madness that come with the craft.

# 44

## Why did the author go broke?

## Because he couldn't make both ends meet!

## 45

What did the grammar book say to the author?

"I'm here to help you, comma and get it!"

## 46

Why do authors always carry a pencil and paper?

Because they can't resist the draw!

## 47

## How do authors greet each other?

"Hey, write on time!"

**48**

## How do authors like their coffee?

## With a plot twist of caffeine!

## 49

# Why did the author write a book about sewing?

She wanted to weave a tale of thread and error!

## 50

## What did the author say when he finished his novel?

“The end, period!”

# 51

## How do you make an author laugh?

## Just give them a good book review!

**52**

Why did the author become a beekeeper?

He wanted to create buzz-worthy stories!

## 53

## Why did the author become a gardener?

## He loved growing plots and characters!

## 54

## What do you call a group of authors competing in a marathon?

A "book" club!

## 55

## What did the author say to the editor who changed his words?

"You're crossing the line, but I'll rewrite it!"

## 56

## How do Authors relax?

They Spend hours staring at a blank page, waiting for inspiration to strike, and then end up binge-watching Netflix instead.

## 57

# How do authors come up with passwords?

They use their characters' names as passwords because they can't remember anything else.

# 58

## What do authors do in public?

They talk to themselves while writing dialogue, often getting strange looks from people nearby.

**59**

# How can you spot an author in a park?

They have imaginary arguments with their characters, sometimes even losing the argument.

## 60

Why did the wife get mad at her husband?

He accidentally called her by the name of one of the characters in his book.

## 61

Why was the author sad?

She got emotionally attached to her fictional character, even mourning his death.

## 62

# Why did the author miss his flight?

He got lost in his own stories and forgot what day it was or where he was supposed to be going.

## 63

# What do authors do during a hurricane?

They hoard pens and notebooks.

## 64

# How do authors procrastinate?

They spend more time researching obscure facts than actually writing the story.

## 65

## What is an author's biggest problem?

They have a love-hate relationship with their own writing, often thinking their work is brilliant one minute and utter garbage the next.

## 66

# Why do authors have pets?

To have someone to talk to as if their pets are trusted writing companions, asking for their opinions on plot twists.

## 67

## What makes an author excited?

When they find the perfect word or phrase, they celebrate it like they won the lottery.

## 68

# What is an author's fetish?

They have a love affair with their bookshelves, spending hours arranging and rearranging their collection.

# 69

## How can you tell when an author is having writers-block?

They get distracted by random ideas and start multiple projects simultaneously, leaving most of them unfinished.

## 70

# What drives an author crazy?

Having intense debates with themselves about whether to use the Oxford comma or not.

## 71

## Why didn't the author sleep in 3 days?

He was overanalyzing every single word and sentence, driving himself crazy with perfection.

## 72

# How did the author spend his vacation?

He created elaborate backstories for random strangers on the street, just for the fun of it.

## 73

## What is an author's secret manipulation?

They use their writing as an excuse to procrastinate on other tasks they don't want to do.

# 74

## How did the author spend her weekend?

She had intense debates with herself over the proper placement of a comma or the perfect synonym for a word.

## 75

## What do authors do for fun?

They look up the most bizarre and random things on the internet in the name of "research."

## 76

# How do authors see characters in their books?

They see their characters as if they are real people, referring to them as their "friends" or "family."

**77**

What do authors do when they have writer's block?

They talk to inanimate objects, asking for inspiration or advice.

## 78

## What would you find under an author's bed?

A never-ending list of story ideas, notebooks filled with plots that may never see the light of day.

# 79

## What gives an author satisfaction when reading books?

Finding a typo or grammatical error in published books, feeling a strange sense of satisfaction in spotting them.

## 80

# What is an author's superpower?

Being able to write entire paragraphs or chapters while half-asleep.

## 81

# Why did the author go broke?

Because he lost his "write" of passage!

## 82

# What do you call an author who can't spell?

A "type-o" writer!

## 83

What do you call an author who can't come up with new ideas?

A "novel"ist!

## 84

# How did the author become a best-selling novelist?

# They "wrote" their way to the top!

## 85

# What is an author's weakness? They can't resist the temptation to eavesdrop on conversations, taking mental notes for future character dialogue.

# 86

## What do you call an author who can't stop daydreaming? A "word" wanderer!

## 87

# Why did the author always carry a thesaurus? Because they wanted to find the "write" words!

## 88

## What did the author say when their book got rejected?

"Guess I'll just have to write them a 'novel' email explaining why they're wrong!"

## 89

How did the author become a master of suspense? They kept their readers "on the edge of the page!"

## 90

How do authors like their coffee?

With a "plot" of cream and a dash of imagination.

# WORDS OF WISDOM FROM FAMOUS AUTHORS

1. "The first draft is just you - telling yourself the story."

*TERRY PRATCHETT*

2. "Write what should not be forgotten."

*ISABEL ALLENDE*

3. "There is no greater agony than bearing an untold story inside you."

*MAYA ANGELOU*

4. "The scariest moment is always just before you start."

*STEPHEN KING*

5. "A writer is someone for whom writing is more difficult than it is for other people."

*THOMAS MANN*

6. "If there's a book that you want to read, but it hasn't been written yet, then you must write it."

*TONI MORRISON*

7. "The beautiful part of writing is that you don't have to get it right the first time."

*JODI PICOULT*

8. "Writing is the painting of the voice."

*VOLTAIRE*

9. "Don't tell me the moon is shining; show me the glint of light on broken glass."

*ANTON CHEKHOV*

10. "The only way to do great work is to love what you do."

*STEVE JOBS*

# 10 THINGS THAT AUTHORS TEACH US

1. **The power of imagination:** Writers remind us of the limitless potential of our imagination and encourage us to explore new worlds and ideas through their stories.
2. **The importance of empathy:** Through their characters and narratives, writers teach us to understand and empathize with different perspectives, fostering compassion and understanding in our own lives.
3. **The beauty of storytelling:** Writers show us the art of crafting compelling narratives that entertain, inspire, and resonate with readers, reminding us of the timeless allure of a well-told story.

4. **The value of self-expression:** Writers encourage us to find our unique voice and express ourselves authentically, reminding us that our stories and experiences matter.
5. **The art of observation:** Writers have a keen eye for detail and teach us to observe the world around us, finding inspiration in the small and ordinary moments of life.
6. **The power of words:** Writers demonstrate the power of language and words, showing us how they can evoke emotions, challenge beliefs, and shape our understanding of the world.
7. **The importance of perseverance:** Writers face numerous challenges in their craft, teaching us the value of persistence, discipline, and resilience in pursuing our passions and goals.
8. **The exploration of human nature:** Writers delve into the complexities of human behavior,

thoughts, and emotions, helping us to better understand ourselves and the world we live in.

9. **The art of revision:** Writers teach us that writing is a process, emphasizing the importance of editing, revising, and refining our work to improve its quality and impact.
10. **The invitation to dream:** Writers inspire us to dream big, to envision a better future, and to believe in the power of our imagination and creativity.

# 10 SENTENCES THAT REMIND US THAT WE ARE ALL AUTHORS

1. Every day, we write our own stories through the choices we make and the actions we take.

2. Our thoughts and emotions are the ink that fills the pages of our personal narratives.

3. The words we speak and the conversations we have shape the plotlines of our relationships and connections with others.

4. Each experience, whether mundane or extraordinary, contributes to the chapters of our unique life story.

5. We have the power to rewrite our narratives, learn from our past, and create a future that aligns with our aspirations.

6. Like writers, we have the ability to craft our own voice and express our ideas and beliefs.

7. Our dreams and goals are the plot twists that add excitement and purpose to our journey.

8. Just as writers face challenges and setbacks, we too encounter obstacles that test our resilience and determination.

9. Through reflection and self-discovery, we can uncover the themes and motifs that define our personal narratives.

10. Ultimately, we are the authors of our own lives, continuously writing and rewriting the story of who we are and who we want to become.

www.ingramcontent.com/pod-product-compliance
Lightning Source LLC
Chambersburg PA
CBHW041558160726
48006CB00042B/2151

* 9 7 9 8 8 6 9 1 8 1 5 0 3 *